THE BIRD IS GONE

A ~~MONOGRAPH~~ *Manifesto*

THE BIRD IS GONE
A ~~MONOGRAPH~~ Manifesto

STEPHEN GRAHAM JONES

FC2
Normal / Tallahassee

Published by FC2 with support provided by Florida State University, the Unit for Contemporary Literature of the Department of English at Illinois State University, the Illinois Arts Council, the Florida Arts Council of the Florida Division of Cultural Affairs, and the National Endowment for the Arts

Address all inquiries to: Fiction Collective Two, Florida State University, c/o English Department, Tallahassee, FL 32306-1580

ISBN: Paper, 1-57366-109-0

Library of Congress Cataloging-in-Publication Data
Jones, Stephen Graham, 1972-
  The bird is gone : a manifesto / Stephen Graham Jones.-- 1st ed.
    p. cm.
  ISBN 1-57366-109-0
  1. Indians of North America--Government relations--Fiction. 2. Restoration ecology--Fiction. 3. Bowling alleys--Fiction. 4. Great Plains--Fiction. I. Title.
  PS3560.O5395B57 2003
  813'.6--dc21
                                    2003002752

Cover Design: Victor Mingovits
Book Design: Laine Morreau and Tara Reeser

Produced and printed in the United States of America
Printed on recycled paper with soy ink

This program is partially supported by a grant from the Illinois Arts Council

NATIONAL
ENDOWMENT
FOR THE ARTS

for Rebecca, mi madre

and for Pidgin

without Brenda Mills to edit it, and get lost in it, and find me in there, pull me out, *Bird* would have never been anywhere, much less gone. and I may never have even finished starting it if Kate Garrick—agent, shield, translator—hadn't said something about how 'this could be good.' and it never would have looked like it looks if Tara Reeser hadn't traded parts of herself in for it. thanks too to Joe Ferrer, for the pointing, the clicking, and to the National Endowment for the Arts and the Texas Writers League, for money, and faith. and to Nancy, still my girlfriend, for listening to me write all night for too many nights in a row.

we only become what we are by the radical
and deep seated refusal of that which others
have made of us

JEAN-PAUL SARTRE

we have taken a new home, and we must
exhaust the past before we can finish with the
present

SAMUEL DELANY

pink eye was all the rage.

LP DEAL, five-ten in boots, but then he can't wear boots at work, either, as part of his job is traipsing down the alleys to retrieve busted pins, motionless balls, the occasional beer bottle. Once, a prosthetic arm. Fool's Hip gives mercy strikes if your arm falls off mid-bowl, but the limit is three per game; some of the veterans were taking advantage. LP tried wearing a pair of the house moccasins when he first signed on, hand-sewn the old way, from the soft leather interiors of thousands of abandoned golf bags, but found he couldn't stand up on the waxed lanes. It was funny for a while, but then he had work to do. Now he wears simple canvas basketball shoes—standard Indian issue—dingy grey at the toes from mopping afterhours, and monochromatic coveralls, once brown but long since gone tan, from washing them every night in the dishwasher with the last load of the night, steam filling the room, scouring his lungs. Sometimes, standing there naked and blurry, he sings, his voice resounding off the stainless steel kitchen, over the polished counter, spilling out into the hardwood lanes, but then other times he just stares at his indistinct reflection, the roadburn all down his left side expanding in the heat.

On his application for employment, under Tribal Affiliation, he checked Anasazi—a box he had to draw himself—and under the story and circumstances of his name, he recounted what he could remember of the Skin Parade fourteen years ago, when he was twelve. He and his mom had been hunting and gathering at the supermart in Hoopa, California when the wall of television sets said it, that the Dakotas were Indian again, look out, and three weeks and two and a half cars later, LP and his mom rolled across the Little Missouri at Camp Crook with nearly four million other Indians. It wasn't the Little Missouri anymore, though, but something hard to pronounce, in Lakota. The grass was still black then, from the fires[1]. When LP and his mom ran out of gas they just coasted through town, and when they finally rolled to a stop, it was in front of a record store, fluorescent letters splashed onto the plate glass. For a moment LP could have been either LP Deal or Vinyl Daze, but then in a rush of nostalgia his mom took the second name. Within a week the guys at the bar were calling her VD. LP didn't get it until years later, months after he'd lost track of her at a pandance, and by then he was old enough to pretend not to care.

He did cut his hair off when he got home that night, though, part of the Code, and hasn't let it grow back yet, wears it blocked off at the collar instead, muskrat-slick on top. His right hand is

---

[1] see INDIAN BURN ('Terms,' p. 166).

forever greasy from smoothing it back, out of his eyes. Mary Boy, LP's boss, offered him a hairnet in passing once, but LP declined: by then he'd grown accustomed to the ducking motion necessary to smooth it down. Had come to depend on it, even, as cover for leaning down to the inside of his left wrist, speaking into the microphone carefully band-aided there, its delicate lead snaking up his arm, embracing his shattered ribcage, plugging into the wafer-thin recording unit tucked into the inner pocket of his overalls.

At night, in his cot in the supply closet by the arcade, the cuticles of his toes still burning from the ammonia and bleach and creekwater of mopping, LP unwinds himself from the mic, jacks an earphone into the recorder, and transcribes his notes feverishly. That's how manifestos are written: with fever. Anything less would be trivial, not worth slogging through concessions and lane duty by day, guarding the place at night. Mary Boy offered him the security gig when he noticed LP had taken up residence at Fool's Hip. LP is pale from it, sunless; he hasn't stepped outside Fool's Hip for seven months—moons, they're called now. It's all the same. Another part of his job is scraping graffiti off the bathroom stalls, both men's and women's.

On one of the stalls in the men's bathroom, like clockwork, there are always suggestions to LP, likely from Mary Boy, adopting some indirect managerial tactic or another. He copies them all into his manifesto. One of them was *why don't you grow your hair like a real Indian?* The time LP found that, he stayed up all night answering it in his notebook, then erased it all before morning, even recarved the question into the stall, to pretend he hadn't seen it. Maybe it wasn't for him. Maybe it wasn't even Mary Boy.

The manifesto is margin to margin, front and back, no spaces between the words, like one long, strained utterance. LP would write on the sides of the paper if he could get his pencil sharp enough. Part of his salary is in notebooks smuggled over from the gift shop. The rest is the cot, thirty free frames a week, and whatever he eats, drinks, and displaces, which isn't supposed to include the video games he plays the old way—with a holy quarter and some braided sinew. What Mary Boy doesn't know he doesn't have to ride his employees about, though. Just let him go on thinking the sweat beaded on LP's forehead in the mornings is from work, from a stubborn piece of gum under one of the bucket seats or something. The lie that works best for LP is that he was just realigning the adhesive arrowheads that point down each lane, *sir*, which both gets Mary Boy waving the *sir* off and appreciating the arrowheads—how they're all just a little off-center, just pointing in the general *direction* of the pins, which will skew the regulars' shots off enough to get them compensating with beer, three dentalia a pitcher. By this time in the conversation the sweat beaded along LP's hairline is a dim memory for Mary Boy, ticking mental shells off three at a time.

Sometimes, too, LP doesn't have to lie about the sweat, if it's hot and dry and the Councilmen are making their rounds from band to band. Then the suggestion LP gets from the bathroom stall is *why not get all the arrows back to factory specs, so the Councilmen can break 230?* For the good of the Nation. LP's been part of it for fourteen years now. He knows how to dig ritual cornmeal from the gutters of the ball return, what songs to mumble while doing it. He knows how to look away respectfully when his people pour the tops of their beers off, for the dead. They're thirsty too, everyone is, even LP.

He doesn't let himself drink, though: his work is too important. Part of writing a manifesto in small, angry letters is being able to read what you've written, at least focus on the print. Another part, apparently, is celibacy. Or, one way to deal with celibacy is to write a manifesto in small, angry letters.

It doesn't matter to LP anymore. He hammers at the buttons of the video games in the predawn hours and no one's there to hear him sing down the lanes, vault from tabletop to tabletop and into the carpeted wall, his reflection still caught in the stainless-steel kitchen.

He keeps his stack of notebooks in one of the lockers and never goes near it during work. The best security is pretending you don't have anything to hide, that you're just a broompusher with a skin condition, a roadburn LP has yet to wholly account for in his manifesto.

MARY BOY, rumored to be acting roadman for the local Red Catholic carryovers. Thus the name. He's never up at Fool's Hip around vespers, anyway, which is suspicious enough. Other than that, he's just an old Winnebego with a greystreaked ponytail and permanent sunglasses, a shady habit he picked up from the FBI, the way he tells it, though he doesn't have any cool federal tattoos to back it up, just a partial one of Jesus' head, high on his right shoulder, signed by a Permanent Inc. studio, OK City, Oklahoma. Back when there was an Oklahoma. The tattoo is proof of that, at least.

Twelve years ago, though, it also counted as proof of Mary Boy's Red Catholic status, which meant he was bowling alone at Fool's Hip, knocking one or two pins over at a time, mentally preparing himself for the ride the sandy-haired pool players said he was going to take with them sooner or later, if he wanted to woo the clan-bowlers into thinking he was one of them—that he was traditional enough to understand the maniacally strict family lines they observed, traditional enough *not* to decorate his body with the image of a white messiah. It was the second worst car experience Mary Boy ever had—the pool players holding him out the open door at a screaming ninety miles per hour, letting his right shoulder skim the asphalt, Mary Boy looking anywhere but down, scanning instead the soundless blur the ditch had become, an out of place black Impala whipping past there, four FBI agents idling around it—one for each direction—their ties testing the midday wind, reminding Mary Boy of the *worst* car experience he ever had.

It was back when he was LP's age, back when you had to burn a tank of gas down to Whiteclay just to get a 12-pack. Back when the FBI could still park on the side of the road and wave Indians over, on the pretense that some crime had allowed them jurisdiction. Mary Boy watched them and their unmarked Impala from the top of the hill, sucked on a shiny new 1984 penny to get his breath legal. It was now or never. And maybe they were just trading plastic beads or something anyway, right?

Mary Boy had enough of those already. He turned his lights off, laid down in the seat, and hurtled past the FBI.

Half a 12-pack later he had to do it again, though.

This time their Impala was across the road, too, pointing at DC for authority. Mary Boy kept both hands on the wheel, in plain sight, and, in answer to the question they hadn't asked yet, told them he didn't know any Junior, and he wasn't there that night, and the way he remembered it, the BIA office always fertilized with manure anyway, somebody probably just backed that dumptruck up too far. When he smiled, copper rained down from his mouth and pooled in his lap.

The FBI at Mary Boy's window smiled back, held a single peyote button up between his thumb and forefinger, as if he were focusing through it. At Mary Boy. They were looking for volunteers, see. And Mary Boy fit the profile. It was all part of a government-funded study: for incarceration purposes, DC needed to establish at what point after ingesting peyote religious experience began for a fully-matured male specimen of the Sioux tribe, and how long that experience lasted—when that inmate could rejoin population. Mary Boy didn't correct them about the Sioux-thing; it's always best to be a member of whatever tribe you're visiting, anyway. Less paperwork for all involved. The button didn't look right, though. Mary Boy directed his chin over to the scrotum hanging from his rearview mirror, told them he had his own, thanks, but they shook their heads no, said this was the one.

Mary Boy swallowed it whole, to delay the effect, fuck with the government.

Years later a visiting geochemist with a taste for bowling alley fare would detail how A) there's no telling what psychotropic reaction might have occurred between the residual copper in Mary Boy's saliva and the peyote; B) it probably wasn't even peyote in the first place, the government just needed a native guinea pig; and C) if it really was a study, there should have been more participants. There were: driving back to Pine Ridge after the requisite one-hour waiting period the study demanded, still waiting for it to kick in, Mary Boy could just make out the other volunteers' headlights, bouncing through the pastures, stalling out, their cars falling even more apart than they already were, rusting into the ground already, grass growing up through the frames. By now all six cylinders of Mary Boy's car had wet hide stretched over them, a little man in full regalia running between, drumming Mary Boy on, faster, faster.

Mary Boy eased his foot down, and the night accelerated around him. Two yellow horses with riders pulled alongside the passenger door, two tempera blue on the driver's side, hooves unplanting great clumps of asphalt. In the rearview mirror were twin black horses with chalky white riders, faces bisected with fingerwide lines of red. It was an escort. Before Mary Boy had time to ask *escort to where?* there was a one-man Civil War reenactment taking place in front of him, some behind-the-lines stuff: an old, thick soldier arcing a delicate line of pee into the tall grass, one hand on his hip, the other clutching the clear neck of a bottle, the rest of him swaying in the headlights.

The six riders and their six horses had become a spectrum of cartoon decals in Mary Boy's peripheral vision by now. His bumper kissed the soldier's shin, and the soldier relaxed his grip on the bottle. It shattered on its way down. Soon enough Mary Boy was loading the soldier's limp body up onto the hood, hooking his spurs into the grille to keep him in place. So he was cavalry.

Mary Boy dug out two beers, had to show the soldier—the *cavalry*man—how to open his. Halfway through it, the cavalryman started crying and trying not to, though, then just slammed the rest of his beer like a modern man, started grubbing for more. When his hat fell over his eyes he brushed it off, and it fell in the lights of the car, and around the crown, still fresh, still bleeding, was some part of a woman.

The cavalryman laughed self-consciously, as if this was just a social error, then tried to stand, fell facefirst into the grass, his spurs still lodged in the elaborate grill.

Some part of an Indian woman.

The headlights dimmed for a moment as Mary Boy started the car, and then he eased into first. The cavalryman was already screaming, enumerating his crimes just to apologize for them more efficiently, *not* wanting to have this horseless carriage driven up his tight, nineteenth-century ass. But Mary Boy had read about hats decorated like that. Whole columns of them. The cavalryman kept up, hand over hand, for nearly a quarter mile, Mary Boy driving with one wrist over the wheel, his door open, taking long, deliberate steps with his left foot.

When the cavalryman finally gave up, Mary Boy was slow getting his left foot in and over to the brake. He rolled the cavalryman over and the cavalryman's mouth was packed with prairie dirt—with Indian land.

Instead of asking him what it tasted like, if he wanted any more, Mary Boy kicked him awake, rested the steel shank of his boot over the cavalryman's trachea. The cavalryman was already gagging, patting himself down for something: a sheet of folded cotton parchment, halogen white in the headlights. The only unsoiled thing on him.

Mary Boy didn't get it, and then he did, tore the paper away and wrote it out himself, with all the clauses and terminology he'd had used against him over the course of two divorces and a string of misdemeanor hearings—that DC was hereby giving back all the Indian land it ever took, would take, or was presently taking.

He flourished his signature across the bottom of the page, corner to corner, then raised his boot so the cavalryman could sign too. The cavalryman climbed the front of the car, leaned over the hood, and scratched his name in ink below Mary Boy's, and with the final letter (*n*) something changed. In the ground. A deep rumbling.

Mary Boy looked away from the cavalryman for a moment and there were headlights, millions of them, streaming towards the Dakotas.

In their glow he gave the treaty a closer look, but the peyote had stripped his letter-sense. He couldn't even tell what he had written, much less make out the cavalryman's slurred signature. 'Forget it,' Mary Boy said to himself finally, reclining his seat to sleep it off, and he did manage to forget it, until it all came true a few years later—the Conservation Act, the Skin Parade, the Red Tide—only Mary Boy had never got around to telling anybody his vision, about waking in a bright field the next morning, an impossibly tall FBI agent taking off his own black shades, passing them down to Mary Boy, whose pupils never recontracted again.

The only people he ever told, besides his daughter, Courtney, who thought it was convenient to relate visions after the fact, were the sandy-haired pool players, who had no black Impala in their short-term memory, and no other kind of memory to go on. They were having a hard enough time remembering how to get from IHS back to Fool's Hip. Mary Boy shook his head no and crossed himself with his bleeding arm when they asked if he had any more tattoos, then stood in the parking lot surveying these Indian Territories he'd signed into existence one night on the way back from Whiteclay. It didn't matter that nobody believed him. The proof was all around.

COURTNEY PELTDOWNE, the one they made the word *svelte* up for. And *lithe*. And *lissom*. All Indian black hair and painted-on jeans, pacing Fool's Hip in her cfm shoes, ashing in the thumbhole of whatever ball's handy, knowing her dad won't call her on it, because then she could rebuild *William* and *Sherman* around the holy *Tecumsah* he claims to remember from his vision, tell the skittish clan-bowlers that that's where he is every dusk—trying to sing the old general up, conjure the Indian Wars all over again. Which is worse than just being a carryover Catholic.

Not that she ever would. Not that she'd ever let Mary Boy know she wouldn't. Fool's Hip is about the last place she has left. Outside its cinderblock walls she's ordinary, one of five million other Indian women. Used to, she could walk into any dancehall in the Dakotas and pretty much shut the place down just by weaving her way to the bar. She was everything exotic; white men held their breath in her presence, passed out at her feet, and she walked over them. Now the closest thing she has to a white man is LP—Scab Boy, she calls him, because of how he looked when he hired on, half his body raw and inflamed, still gauzed under his coveralls.

All these Indians.

God.

Everything that used to set Courtney apart is standard now—skin, hair, mannerisms; history. She goes to the exchange and sees herself behind the counter, in line, in the parking lot, and sometimes has to run away. To Fool's Hip, to Scab Boy. To talk to him in sultrysad tones and mouth her cigarette until his coveralls become a tent, the sign for her to spill her drink, watch him try to clean it up without swinging his hard-on into the side of the table. It's the small amusements, she tells herself, but knows it's more: the first night after Mary Boy took her key away, she found herself standing at the entry door, cupping her hands against the glass, the arcade darkened, Scab Boy's closet a rectangle of light, thicker at the bottom because there wasn't carpet anymore, but tile.

She didn't ring the buzzer, just watched, let her hands relax until she could see herself in the dark glass—thirty-four and fiercely beautiful, standing out in the cold to monitor the nocturnal activities of a broompusher who doesn't even have a second change of clothes, who talks down his sleeve and then writes deep into the morning on notebooks he's obviously keeping in locker 32b. Everybody knows. Until the dishes of lunchtime, the downside of his right hand will be smudged so heavy with pencil lead, it'll rub off on the video games, like he's leaving his shadow behind.

For Mary Boy to find. But Mary Boy never does. It's always gone before he gets there—on the same napkin as Courtney's lipstick. Because Scab Boy can't get caught: he might be writing about her, Courtney. Which is why she supplies him with notebooks pilfered from the dock of the exchange, why she corners him throughout the day, supplying him with details about herself. How *Peltdowne* is just what her great-grandmother's name translated out as on the 1907 rolls. How she was a vegetarian until Indian Days started fourteen years ago, and salad was suddenly Anglo, not on any of the menus.

For two weeks she starved, living on beer and frybread with everybody else, but finally, alone after Mary Boy had left the trailer for the morning, she pinched the edges off of the deer sausage he'd left on the counter until there was nothing left, and then she was defrosting everything in the freezer, slabs of new buffalo dissolving in her mouth, grease running down her chin like the bow and arrow days.

God.

Sometimes she has to tell herself not to laugh. To take all this seriously. But sometimes it's better to just pretend, too. That this really is all Mary Boy's dream. But then she's there again, at the locked door of Fool's Hip, her hands cupped to the glass, and next she's walking away, the box of notebooks behind her, fluttering in the wind. And at night the Territories are so empty. She understands why Scab Boy never goes outside. She walks along the fence all the way back to the trailer, holding on so she won't disappear, and when the fence is gone she runs from mile marker to mile marker, telling herself not to look to either side, not to believe the stories—that the Old Ones are out there on their unshod horses, with their lances and their scalps and their downturned mouths. Watching. Waiting. Not saying anything yet.

But they know, can see Courtney in that Havre bar when the radio said it, about the Conservation Act, can see how she instinctively cast around for another Indian, to share this with, found herself alone. Made do eventually with the German roughneck, whose fingers were still showing blue on her side five days later, but at the moment she didn't know what he was capable of, just draped herself over him, paying her own quarters for the songs, the bartender angling the floodlight onto them, this one last dance.

It was worth it.

NICKEL EYE, Salishan, primary suspect in the disappearance of thirty-nine Anglo tourists, one at a time, three a year since he showed up in the Territories. Fool's Hip is his running alibi, though—the permanent slump in his back from sitting at the bar day in day out, how the tips of his unbraided hair have taken on the citrus-smell of whatever LP uses to wipe the counter down. His acquired ability to tell how many pins a bowler's knocked down, going solely by the sound they make, crashing up the alley, into the kitchen, over the counter, washing over him.

He doesn't pay for his draft with dentalia or blankets or hides, either, like the rest of the Skins, but with crisp Anglo bills. Which is why the tribal police questioned him about the missing tourists. It was a Thursday; one of them had a crackling radio squelched into some pocket, and they both had big, obvious sidearms.

'So,' Detective Blue Plume led off, doing something official with his chrome-tipped boots, leaning over Nickel Eye's section of the bar, 'between us, where you keeping them?'

Nickel Eye shrugged, pretended not to notice Special Agent Chassis Jones at his drinking arm. They had him surrounded. 'Them?'

Chassis Jones' face creaked when she smiled. 'Full sentences, please, Nikolai.'

'It's Nickel *Eye*.'

'Niko*lai*,' she repeated, staring him down in the mirror.

Nickel Eye shook his head. 'Didn't quite get that,' he said, moving his mouth more than he had to. 'Could you rephrase it in a full sentence maybe?' The curved rim of his mug almost fit his smile. Blue Plume's boot rotated his stool away from Chassis Jones.

'Whatever,' Blue Plume said about the name. 'Answer the question.'

'About 'them.''

Blue Plume nodded.

'With a longer sentence, too,' Chassis Jones added.

Nickel Eye winked at Mary Boy, said 'nyet.' But Mary Boy didn't smile back, just directed Nickel Eye back into the interrogation. Chassis Jones was waiting, 'Listen Nickel *Eye*,' she said. 'We can do this the easy way or—'

'You mean you can still even *use* that line?' Nickel Eye asked, and when Blue Plume stood to his full height he waved him back down, spoke to him instead of Chassis Jones. 'Between us,' he said in his best stage whisper, 'where am I keeping who?'

'*Whom*,' Blue Plume corrected, 'it's where are you keeping *whom*.'

Nickel Eye leaned back, crossed his ankles. 'That's pretty much what I want to know, Detective.'

'You're going to pull an eyebrow muscle like that,' Chassis Jones said.

'Those thirty-three American tourists,' Blue Plume said. 'That's who.'

'*Whom*,' Nickel Eye tried, but Chassis Jones told him not to get cute. He told her it was too late, and maybe he was a trickster anyway, right?

'Like we don't hear that one every Saturday night.'

Blue Plume rolled his eyes.

'But really,' Nickel Eye said. 'How many seventh cavalrymen does it take to screw in a lightbulb?'

'We're not that easy,' Chassis Jones said back.

'And it's not late enough in the afternoon for me to say thirty-nine, *Chassis*.'

'Special Agent Jones, thank you. For giving yourself away too.'

Nickel Eye made a show of looking at his watch: 4:48. 'Oops,' he slurred, then tried to make the cut-off sign to Blue Plume, where Chassis Jones wouldn't see, meaning it takes *no* seventh cavalrymen to screw a lightbulb into place. After some official eye contact with Chassis Jones, Blue Plume nodded back to Nickel Eye that he got it, yes. But he wasn't laughing.

'Only the kidnapper would know it was thirty-nine,' Chassis Jones said. 'Textbook.'

'Kidnapper?'

'You used the present tense. 'Where *am* I keeping them.''

'Shit,' Nickel Eye said, ruminating his beer. 'I thought I was just a damn serial killer. Man. What do you feed Americans anyway? Hypothetically, I mean. Wait, wait. Land, right? An acre for breakfast, two for lunch...?'

'I don't expect you to tell me where they are,' Chassis Jones said, packing up.

'But you'll be watching me,' Nickel Eye said, wagging a finger between her and Blue Plume. 'You two ace detec—...'

'No,' Blue Plume said, 'just go about your daily business.'

Here Nickel Eye held his beer up to the light, toasted them out the door, whistled for Mary Boy and wiped his forehead. Behind him, Denim Horse knocked down a spare—6\9\10, from catching the headpin at too steep an angle it sounded like, hooking too sharp to the left, hanging it all out over the gutter, showing off: Denim Horse's weakness. Courtney must be in the pit.

Nickel Eye knows them all so well, Mary Boy included. Their game is for Nickel Eye to order a beer on the house, for Mary Boy to shake his head no, then for Nickel Eye to straighten his BDU jacket at the collar, threaten to pack up his dolls and go home. It's not like he doesn't have the money, though, which finally pulled the tribal dicks—as he was already calling them—back up for part 2 of interrogation 1. They caught him just after lunch, so it was all much more casual; he called them Dick and Miss Dick, and they called him Killer, let him sit up front, shoulder to shoulder.

'Where to?' he asked, looking side to side at each of them, and then they were there, Broken Leg, a prairie-dog town that drifted for miles.

'Target practice,' Blue Plume said, then fastdrew on one just as it peeked out of its hole, blew it six feet in the air, the highest it had ever been, probably.

'Miss Dick...?' Nickel Eye asked, voice betraying him, but Chassis Jones was already lining up on one over the hood. Nickel Eye leaned on the trunk just as she was breathing out, pulled the shot high. A brown fan rose behind the prairie dog.

'I could do this all day,' he said to her, then quit smiling all at once: the butt of Blue Plume's pistol was suddenly and undeniably in his hand. It weighed as much as his whole arm.

'Your turn,' he said, but Nickel Eye shook his head no.

Chassis Jones lifted his gun arm for him when he couldn't, from the elbow. 'Just the same as with the tourists, Killer,' she said, 'go on. It's easy.'

She pushed him out, towards them.

'No,' he was still saying.

'So it's *not* like the tourists?' Blue Plume prompted, and Nickel Eye shook his head no, no, even said it: that these prairie dogs hadn't done anything *wrong*, see?

Blue Plume's recording unit clicked off, satisfied, and the sound pushed Nickel Eye around, the pistol still at arm-level. He was holding it loosely, unsure what he was going to do. What he could do: anything. Chassis Jones wavered in the peep sight, the bead resting heavy on her sternum, but Nickel Eye couldn't do it finally, couldn't pull the trigger, was suddenly afraid of the pistol kicking up through the heel of his hand and into his ulna, his own sternum. 'No,' he said again, then started backing away, stumbling into hole after hole, finally turning to run. When the Dick car was a speck, he dropped Blue Plume's pistol into a hole, scaring an owl awake, and by the time he sidled back up to the bar at Fool's Hip he was shiny with sweat, holding his stomach, shaking.

He looked to Mary Boy and Mary Boy looked back, topped off a mug, knocked on the bar for the first time ever, but Nickel Eye had the stomach of his shirt too full with blind prairie-dog pups to raise the beer. And he was yelling, anyway—the end of the joke, that it didn't take *any* seventh cavalrymen to screw in a lightbulb, because they don't *need* any goddamn lightbulbs in hell.

Two weeks later, Special Agent Chassis Jones went missing.

DENIM HORSE, the kind of Lakota that would have been kidnapped for the movies twenty years ago, just on principle, just because his black braids and chiseled face fit with the shirtless Indians of romance-book covers. Now, instead of being a movie star, he's a bowling pro. He does stand by the box fan sometimes, though, down by lane 15, arms crossed, eyes fixed on some middle distance, as if he was born too late, shouldn't really be here. The tourists can't get enough of him. He hasn't bought his own lunch in ten months, since before LP started working at Fool's Hip, and then it was just to prove to Courtney that he could, yes. He wasn't just some pow-wow circuit reject. She pretended not to notice; Denim Horse pretended not to care. The anthropologist on the Aborigine Hotline said it was a courting ritual of the Plain Indian.

'*Plains*,' Denim Horse corrected at three American dollars a minute, fed into the payphone one quarter at a time, and then for free the anthropologist shook his head audibly, no: *plain*. Denim Horse was still flipping off the mouthpiece of the receiver when Cat Stand walked through the double doors in slow motion, trailing Naitche, her whipthin son, five years old, six maybe, his big eyes cataloging everything in an autistic glance.

'Tell me about her,' the anthropologist said, hungry, but Denim Horse just lowered the phone, reaching for more change, uncounted mounds of it.

He's not even sure when that was, anymore. A year? A month? The days began smearing together about then. He went what felt like three weeks without saying anything to anybody, anyway— just nodding down the lane for the American women bowlers, correcting stances with the hand signals they thought were authentic, keeping Cat and her blistering white teeth in his peripheral vision, where she'd already been for twenty-odd years. The buses pulled in, left again, and still she remained, not saying anything either, Naitche haunting the arcade, living on refresco and dried elk, straight from the jar. Mary Boy let it go. There was something about her, about them.

'So why doesn't she talk, kimo?' the anthropologist nudged Denim Horse, and Denim Horse dropped another quarter, watched Cat across the pit and whispered that he'd grown up with her the first six years of his life, down around Eufala. The anthropologist tried to say something about how life-histories weren't really his department, but Denim Horse was already rolling, desperate, detailing how his dad followed work to Arizona, brought the child Denim Horse was with him, brought him to the Indian rodeo in Aztec eight years later where he caught up with her again, Cat, only now they were both grown, fourteen at least, and looking at each other with different eyes after the final go-round.

She was famous by then, too—the Lactose Tolerant Indian, on all the milk containers, in beaded buckskin—so everybody recognized her. Denim Horse was the only one who knew her well enough to lead her out into the scrub with a blanket, though, talk her shirt off, tell her he'd been thinking about her for eight years now, that it must be true what everybody said about her when she was young, being passed around from relative to relative: that she wasn't like the rest of them. Cat shrugged in a way that her pants fell off, Denim Horse's too. It was second nature now, but then, that was the first time. For both of them. The contract stock snorting and stomping twenty yards away. Denim Horse catching one of his friends' hands reaching in out of the night, to their blanket, then retracting soundlessly.

It had left a glass. Of white. For the Lactose Tolerant Indian.

'Thomas,' Cat said, his name back then, and Denim Horse smiled, studied the simple pattern of the blanket they were on, looked back up. Cat had the glass in both hands. Cat for *Catherine*, he thought. Thomas and Catherine, Catherine and Thomas.

'Shit heads,' he said, about the milk, his friends, the rodeo, the way her eyes were already wet from this joke she couldn't get away from. 'You don't have to,' he told her, but Cat just shrugged, held the glass up to her face. It took her breath away, the milk, and she looked deeper into it, through the bottom of the glass and into the showbarn, whatever kind of cow could have milk this white.

This hot. Her eyes glistened with shame and something else. 'Wha—?' Denim Horse started to ask, but now she was panning up over the rim of the glass, into Denim Horse, just like she did in the commercials he knew by heart. Like this was for him, like she wanted him to see.

'No,' he said, because something was wrong, but before his arm could cross the distance between them she had the glass tilted back. When it was gone she dropped it, wiped the back of her mouth with her forearm, and a single line of watery blood snaked down from her right nostril, around her lip.

'Cat?' Denim Horse asked, '*Catherine*...?' and Cat smiled at this, her name, then collapsed backwards, her naked chest already convulsing.

'It wasn't milk,' the hotline anthropologist figured, putting the quarters in from his end now, and Denim Horse shook his head no, it wasn't: more like bleach. His friends were shit heads, he said again.

'So it's not that she *doesn't* talk,' the anthropologist said, 'it's that she *can't*,' and Denim Horse shrugged. She'd known it wasn't milk. That was the thing. And his name—Thomas. It was the last word she'd said, and no matter the number of white women he got to say it too, under him, straddling him, in the living room the bedroom the bathroom, her voice was still there, always there— *Thomas*, the hiss under his fourteen-pound custom ball as it leans out over the gutter, spinning hard the opposite way, trying to get something back, fine grey ash slinging up evenly from the thumbhole, the pins aware enough in their wooden way to lie down for him. But still he breaks them. The day Cat Stand walked in he splintered twenty-eight in twelve frames, some at the neck, some down the middle, some the old way. It was the closest Fool's Hip had ever been to a perfect game. Lane 15 trembled with anticipation, the whole alley holding its breath for him, but then Denim Horse just stood there on the brink, at the foul line, until finally Mary Boy sidled up beside him, said to take it home maybe, this wasn't how a professional did it.

Denim Horse just held his ball at thigh-level, the fan behind him, the phone across the pit ringing and ringing, Fool's Hip finally getting uncomfortable enough with it that LP swept over, nudged it off the hook, made eye contact with Denim Horse, who looked away, back to Mary Boy. 'I am home,' he told Mary Boy, hours after Fool's Hip had closed, the afterimage of Naitche intense at one of the video games, one eye milky blue, like Denim Horse's is without the contact.

BACK IRON, called Deerboy by some of the clan bowlers, for obvious reasons. When Denim Horse wouldn't lend his profile to the arcade tokens Mary Boy was minting up one summer, Back Iron offered his, held his chin up as high and vain and noble as his twin brother, let Mary Boy set it in alloy and add the braids later. Aside from them—the braids—the only difference between Denim Horse and Back Iron is that Back Iron wears women's clothes and eyeliner, lets Courtney paint his nails, lies to her that he's descended from Roman Nose and American Horse and Nana.

'Some orgy,' Courtney says, never looking up from her file.

'Nineteenth damn century,' Back Iron says back, watching his brother sling the ball down the lane. 'Back when they knew how to *do* it, girl.'

The nails Courtney shapes are false, though, glue-ons. Like the dress and the make-up and the walk, it's part of the disguise, just who Back Iron is in the daylight hours. At night he takes the wig off and runs his palm over his slick-bald head, all he has left of the leukemia that irradiated his early twenties. He's thirty-two now, and the treatments are just a dim glow, what he uses to find his way over electrical fences, across manicured lawns, through impossible skylights and down onto pressure-sensitive floors, into a grid of infrared light.

When he looks back up to where he came from, it's like the old stories, like he uprooted a turnip and there was this skylight, a hole into another world. All he had to do was drop a rope, follow it down into the past, the skulls and drums and beaded warshirts welling up around him, pressed behind humidity-controlled glass, making him rich. More than Denim Horse pulls in, anyway. Not bad for a bald, sterile transvestite.

He tells himself it doesn't matter that he likes the dresses, how sheer his hairless legs look in nylon, standing in line with the rest of the Nation for an assistance check at the first of the month then fanning himself with it at Fool's Hip. Pretending that's all he has, that he doesn't make that much in a single night sometimes, then lose it running from dogs or headlights or the sound of closing doors. Or tribal cops at Fool's Hip in the daytime.

The day they walked in, blinking, shades in hand, Back Iron's mascara almost ran down his face all at once. Did he leave evidence at the museum, an afterglow or something? Had they followed him here with a geiger-counter? Was this some fucking cartoon? Shit shit shit. For the first time ever, he took his wig off in Fool's Hip, stood to his full height, plus whatever the stiletto heels gave him. He walked out of them and indirectly to his neoprene duffle bag, the turtle shell rattles and sandstone pipes and wintercounts rolled up in rubber bands, indicting him, the rattle trembling already with the law so near.

If the cops heard, it was all over. Even if they suspected. Possession of sacred items not local to your tribe was treason, and treason meant exile, a long vanride to the edge of the Territories, to America, the anthropologists massed at the border with their binoculars and their listening devices and their Scalpel-brand pencils, each of them wanting you to confirm their pet theory: if population density belied ancient migratory routes or if they were the leftovers of band solidarity; what postcards looked like these days on the Inside; how the term 'apple' wasn't used for white Indians anymore; whether it was true that the traditionals now— the pullbacks—were the old people clinging to their microwaves and satellite dishes, while the progressives were out in the grassland with their travois and dogs and their Old Ones, refusing even the horses that followed them around. And a hundred other things Back Iron didn't even know or want to know.

He would kill himself first, in the van. There was always a way—the guards always *left* you a way, because they were people too, knew that exile was worse than hanging yourself with a seatbelt, throwing yourself from an open door, swallowing your tongue.

It wouldn't come to that, though. Back Iron wouldn't let it. Not for just one bag of contraband. Without turning around, he rented every locker available, put one relic in each, and then, keeping his back to the cops, to the whole bar, all watching him in bare feet and naked head, he padded into the men's bathroom, denying them all the eye contact they had to be wanting, and flushed every last key, even the one that floated back up. Now the lockers were locked forever. Back Iron leaned against the wall uncaught, nodded to himself in the mirror, and was on his way out again to trade wits with the police when he heard it: a scratching in the far stall.

He stood there for maybe two minutes, trying to think a way out, an excuse for the plastic clatter the keys had made in the bowl, for his sigh that had turned into a laugh when he flushed. It was a groan, now. He opened the door. There on the toilet was the arcade kid, pants around his ankles, and beside him waiting was his mother, toilet paper in hand, John Wayne warholled on every square.

She didn't say anything with her mouth, the mom, but her eyes were full of something, and slowly Back Iron got it: she thought he was Denim Horse. She thought Denim Horse had flushed all the keys. He smiled his best tourist-killing smile and nodded out of the doorway, the air full of apology, mistake, all that.

Back in Fool's Hip the tribal cops were questioning the regulars at the bar, Nickel Eye giving them the run-around it looked like. Back Iron collected his wig and his heels and leaned back in his chair to watch the show, wait for his turn, which never came, just LP Deal, appearing for a moment with a styrofoam cup swimming with rose petals.

'For me?' Back Iron said, touching his chest with his fingertips, but Long Play was already sweeping his way back to the kitchen. And they weren't rose petals, but the false nails that broke off everytime Back Iron straightened his hose or reached into his purse for change. Like he just had, to rent the lockers.

Back Iron laughed out his nose a little, leaned back, studied the ceiling to keep the mascara pooled in his eyes from brimming over. Maybe everybody knew, shit, even Denim Horse, with all his hair and trophies and women.

'You alright, hun?' Courtney asked from her side of the table, girl to girl, and after a few moments Back Iron managed a smile, pointed with the styrofoam cup to the tribal cops.

'I want the tall one,' he whispered, then held his wrists together for him, waited.

CAT STAND, former banner-child for the 'Indian Problem'—lactose intolerance. It was a sham, though: her manager fed her digestive aids by the handful. Some days she would have to drink from seventy-five glasses before the shot was just right, and those nights even the chalky tablets didn't help. She'd fetal up in her trailer and hold her stomach and mumble the few Creek words she remembered from Eufala: *close the door, don't, look*. And the word for milk.

In the commercials she started out as a bright fleck surrounded by grassland, which resolved to a white buffalo calf for a moment before applying the brakes, pulling in too close to the calf's coat, backing off to show the coat was a robe now, one Cat was walking out of on her way to the breakfast table, with seventy-five glasses of milk balanced on it, one at a time. Never any cereal, never any straws, just Dairyland's Indian Princess and pure homogenized goodness. In the last few weeks before Arizona, she'd even had to bind her new breasts in bandages to look wholesome, like the cartoon pictures on the cartons. Her face and torso were on fourteen million gallons across America when she let Denim Horse lead her out into the darkness. They all expired that night.

Denim Horse had been her first and last. She hadn't meant to
ever see him again.

The way she wrote it to the scab at the toll booth a year ago,
Naitche didn't even have a father. It was a lie, though; she just
didn't have enough paper to tell him the full story—waking from
her yearslong Arizona coma to a vision of dyed feathers, mistak-
ing herself for a bird for an instant, except birds don't mate belly
to belly, but running along highwires, eyes fixed miles away, their
feet clenching thousands of ohms for as long as *I love you* lasts. Cat
tried to run too but her heels didn't reach the bedframe, and then
the mattress spasmed and there was a vision of a fancydancer
standing up from her, still in regalia and face paint. She could
taste the paint on her lips. He even had an entry number on still.
Thomas, Cat said, repeated, her only word, but none of the nurses
believed her until she started showing, and then they just whispered and crossed themselves.

She delivered Naitche alone one night in December, her monitor leads dangling, and knew from the way he didn't cry that the
hospital would take him away if she let them. So she didn't. She
held him to her chest and they walked down the sterile halls and
out the front door together, into the snow, into the cab of a plow
crawling out of town.

'You sure?' the driver asked. He didn't see Naitche until the
door was closed, either, but when he did he just nodded, turned
up the heater, found a Christmas station on the radio.

'I won't look,' he said, nodding down to Naitche, and Cat
followed his eyes. Naitche was gumming for her breast in his mute
way. It was like a nature show Cat had seen once with pups or
cubs. And dugs. The driver laughed awkwardly, politely, and something inside Cat dropped, physically *fell*, and she held him close,
Naitche, too close to nurse, and—without looking somehow, like
he said—the driver downshifted and passed over handful after
handful of tiny, sealed buckets of non-dairy creamer. It was
Naitche's first meal. After that it was formula, Cat massaging the
milk from her breasts into toilets, showers, wherever they were,

until the gutters of America ran white and her breasts were so tender flannel was the only thing she could wear. At night in the same bed with Naitche she still remembered saying it—*close the door, don't, look*—only now it was in English: don't look, go away.

The snowplow driver's name was Nathaniel Hybird, Nathaniel H., Nate-H, Naitche. Not Thomas or Denim Horse, just Naitche. When Cat's milk was gone, the flannel remained. It was warm, four layers deep in places, deep enough that she can do her laundry in shifts and never have to be completely naked, like Arizona, the abandoned rodeo grounds smearing past, the night air rushing over her bare skin, drawing the heat from her.

The enamel of her teeth is thin, almost translucent, but the rest of her is a calcium deposit—robust build, thick braid; attitude. There are moments, though. Sometimes at the laundromat with her cupful of colorsafe bleach she'll hesitate, and Naitche will tune into her stillness from his station by the vending machine, and she won't say anything, will just drop the quarter, start the wash again.

'Guess we better call the pope,' the scab at the toll booth had told her a year ago, about Naitche not having a father, but Cat didn't smile with him, because she didn't plan on ever seeing him again—on ever *having* to see him again—even with short hair and a new job, a broom to lean on: LP. Long Play Deal. He doesn't remember her though, or Naitche, the immaculate conception and the phonecall to the Great White Stepfather, just brings her burger after burger, a cow a week probably, on the house, no cheese. Naitche remembers him, of course. He remembers everything.

What happened to your hair? she asked LP once on one of the bathroom stalls, waiting for Naitche to finish, and then changed it to why didn't he grow it like a real Indian? The last time she'd seen him he'd been outside the tollbooth for a busload of tourists, his ear to the asphalt, listening for traffic.

The two letters of his name were all over the arcade until Naitche took over. Now all the high scores are *CAT, CAT, CAT*, burning themselves into the screen, whispering to her that no one's forgotten, that eating ice cream in the dark is still eating ice cream, even if it hurts your teeth in a good and necessary way.

OWEN 82, as in no wins, eighty-two losses. Basketball. He was the first one to call Back Iron *Back Iron*. It was the season they quit calling him *coach* in the tribal papers, started the whole 'Owen82'-thing. During the first few weeks of the Skin Parade—when everyone was still drinking and IHS wasn't set up yet—he tried to get people to call him Second Raise, but it didn't stick. He had lost eighty-two games in one season, even with the Twin Towers on his side, Back Iron and Denim Horse—Thomas and the Prairie Fairy, then. Numbers 45 and 54. Owen82's offense was breaking down man-to-man defenses with likeness, Back Iron stumbling over his feet like Denim Horse then rising in his liquid-phoenix way, melting across half-court for the ball, laying it up soft instead of dunking, like everybody knew he could, like everybody wanted.

The gyms they played in thundered, until the third quarters at least, when some scrappy point guard would take the intentional foul and claw Thomas or his brother's face, marking them for the rest of the game, breaking Owen82's offense down. It never broke down in practice, though, the imaginary crowds streaming down onto the floor after the last buzzer, draping the net over Owen82's neck and carrying him off into oral history.

Sometimes they practiced twice a day.

If he just could have won one, it would have all turned out different. 'Juan 81' maybe. Anything but *O*wen.

The backside of the strip of paper on his chest the day LP walked up to Fool's Hip said that *the end of the trail starts here*. It was already fluttering in the wind; the whistle holding it down wasn't regulation, either. Owen82'd had to turn his official one in when he retired under suspicion, when he couldn't explain how, the year after his no-win season, he got a second chance, suddenly had all the players, the best of the Territories. Denim Horse and Back Iron were graduated by then, of course—Back Iron undergoing therapy in some American hospital, Denim Horse dancing for the crowds at pow-wows all across the northern hemisphere—but Owen82 didn't need them anymore.

His new offense would be about speed, endurance. *Guerilla ball* he called it in the paper, two weeks to the day before he was drummed out. Fool's Hip was a natural replacement: the waxed alleys were hardwood. They felt right, sounded the way a floor should sound. And the Twin Towers were there, too, still as lean and hard and indifferent to each other as they'd ever been. Two sides of the same Indian-head coin. It was how Owen82 had found them again—in a handful of silver from the exchange.

The day LP hired on, Owen82 was stationed at the bar as usual, rolling the coin across the back of the knuckles of his right hand, him and Nickel Eye watching Naitche light another cigarette for his mom, pass it up to her, then look down once at her lane of the day—just *once*—and then up to the pins, telling her with hand motions where Mary Boy had changed the markers last night, where true center was for the day. Nickel Eye nudged Owen82 and all Owen82 could do was laugh, shake his head. If he'd had a kid like Naitche on his side back when, he wouldn't be here now.

That was the day Cat Stand took seven hundred and fifty American dollars from the clan bowlers, her sixteen-pound ball hurtling down the lane, unstoppable and wide. Even Denim Horse had had to watch. It was a clinic almost, until the final frames, when Naitche approached his mom for another token. She turned to him like she didn't recognize him, but then, when she did, took him by the upper arm, led him past the clan bowlers to the bar, sat him on a stool, tiny blue moons already rising from his arm.

'Sorry, man,' Owen82 said to him, the kid, Naitche, about the bruises, and Naitche looked up to him, unrolled a piece of gum that appeared on the bar, and said that about the end of the trail, even gave Owen82 the strip of comic paper that had been wrapped around the gum. They couldn't look away from each other; hours later Naitche was still sitting there, chewing, and it took LP Deal to get him away from the bar, lead him to a corner of the arcade with a blue felt-tip marker, make the tiny blue moons in his upper arm into bear claws. By closing time Nickel Eye had the tattoo too, and Mary Boy, and Eddie Dial the Navajo consultant. Naitche was a star.

The end of the trail he'd said, though.

Owen82 wrote it down letter by letter on the back of one of the strips of paper in his pocket. The rest he would give to the wind.

Sometime after that he drifted out the front doors. Nobody could give the detectives a precise time. One moment he was there, the next he wasn't, and the next after that LP Deal was kneeling over him in a borrow pit, holding still the note on Owen82's chest: *the end of the trail starts here.*

There was a pistol in Owen82's wrong hand and a hole in his stomach.

Because Denim Horse couldn't, Back Iron cried for both of them.

Four hours after his interview with Mary Boy, the words carved in the stall of the men's bathroom were *who killed coach?* That night LP Deal started his manifesto.

why don't you grow your hair like a real Indian?

not now. she's watching.

THE ONLY GOOD INDIAN

PINK EYE was all the rage. It was the new strain: only Indians could get it. Everyone else was white-eyes, pale face, headlights; not to be trusted. But there are ways. There are always ways.

I bought the contacts in America, at the wig store, then got on the bus before dawn, crossed back over the border into Indian Territory. I was undercover now. The sun was so red that morning, my hair so blonde. The American next to me was rolling the spine of a goose feather back and forth between his index finger and thumb, so that it flashed black-and-white, black-and-white, an old movie cupped in his hands.

'You're nostalgic,' I told him, and he nodded, said he used to live here. A house, a garage, a car. The newspaper slapping his front door every morning.

'You're Indian,' he said, touching his own eye instead of mine, and I shrugged, still in disguise.

'Part,' I lied. 'Enough, I guess.'

'It's okay,' he said.

I looked at him.

'I don't hold it against you, I mean,' and then he turned back to the window. Maybe I would point this one out to Nickel Eye, I thought, as bait. Or maybe I wouldn't have to.

'Number forty,' I said, just loud enough.

'Excuse me?'

Nothing. Just Fool's Hip rolling up over the dashboard, a coyote skulking behind the building, black lips pulled back in a satisfied grin.

'What does it mean?' the American asked the bus in general, me in particular.

'You don't know nostalgia,' I said.

'The coyote,' he said. 'It means something, though.'

'You never should have come back, that's what.'

'But I've got to see,' he said, 'Him.' And then he handed me the feather.

I was the last one off the bus, but that was in a minute. First I used one of your tricks, Blue Plume: five American dollars in the tip can.

'*Him?*' I asked.

'Jesus,' the driver grunted, his voice modulating, shifting gears, and then swished the doors closed behind me, blowing my synthetic hair over my face. I don't know what ever happened to that feather.

He was the first one I saw through the glass doors—sitting at the bar in his olive green jacket, the frosted mug glinting through his hair in slender pieces, golden as wheat—and then I didn't look at him for two weeks. It was easy to get lost in Fool's Hip, to lose yourself; to hide. My system adapted to refresco and deer sausage, to smoke and noise, to pins crashing all around, all the time.

The American I rode in with made it out alive, after he saw Mary Boy's shoulder—Jesus' blue face stained with blood, glistening.

'A miracle,' he whispered.

'Call the pope,' I whispered back.

The girls of lane 15 laughed with me. They were all waiting for their turn with Denim Horse. We were a seething, blonde mass. Eddie Dial was my first friend. The Navajo consultant. He was supposed to know how to run a reservation.

'This isn't a reservation,' I told him, an introduction.

'Petting zoo,' he said back quietly, in his clipped way. It was what America called it—us; the Indian Territories. He touched my yellow hair.

'Please,' I said, pulling away.

'You're...' he led off, studying my cheekbones.

'Seminole,' I finished, another lie.

'But so blonde.'

'*Today*,' I said, ashing before I really needed to. Eddie Dial smiled, nodded; accepted me. This is how it's done: not with batting eyelashes or dropped names, but veiled hostility, a casual disregard. 'So who's the Red Indian?' I asked, angling my cigarette to Mary Boy, crossing the pit for the clan bowlers, pitcher in hand.

'His boss,' Eddie Dial said, directing me down to lane 2, LP Deal. Out past the foul line, down on fingertips and toes, ear to the hardwood, eyes closed; listening. This is how I'll always remember him: in the silence of no-one bowling, not even Cat Stand. They were all holding their breath, waiting for him.

Yes, he nodded. Yes yes yes.

Eddie Dial laughed. 'They're coming,' he interpreted for LP, and for a moment I could hear them too: the Councilmen, rolling heavy in their airbrushed El Dorados, Fool's Hip caught in the crosshairs of their hood ornaments, Mary Boy's tattoo large and distorted through the front doors, drawing them in from all four corners.

'How long?' I asked Eddie Dial, but Eddie Dial was gone. Now he was Denim Horse, but not: Back Iron.

'Few days,' he said. 'Maybe a week.'

'And then?'

'And then we won't matter anymore. You mind?'

I shook my head no and he salvaged my cigarette from the ashtray, breathed it in deep then studied it over his red nails. The filter was milky white.

'What do you want?' I asked him, but he just leaned back, exhaled.

'Don't think you have it,' he said, watching Denim Horse, his voice lilting away. 'But I sure do like that dress.'

Three days later he was wearing it, his elbows on the table, Naitche in his lap.

'Hello,' I said to him, Naitche, but he just stared. The muscles of his eyes were still twitching from the arcade. His fingers smelled of sinew and electricity. This was the day his mother rolled 233 three times in a row, head to head with Denim Horse eight lanes down. They were so polite about who got to go first.

'Hello,' I said again, to Naitche.

'Don't bother,' Back Iron said.

When my cigarette went out, though—inattention, a slip— Naitche held it to his lips, ground the lighter, turned his head to exhale.

'Thank you,' I said, taking it between my first and second finger. 'Thank you.' The whole time saying *I'm not her*, *I'm not her*, his mother, Cat Stand. It's easy to lose yourself at Fool's Hip, though. To forget and breathe in once, twice, after meals, pack after pack.

'You should slow down,' Back Iron said once, but Nickel Eye was talking to a tourist at the bar about Mary Boy's bleeding tattoo, and I couldn't. My filters that day were black with nerves.

The night before Special Agent Chassis Jones officially disappeared, she had a dream. Nickel Eye was in it with her. It was whatever season it is when the grass in the cemetery is yellow and loud enough to make you feel like an intruder. Not yellow, though, but golden, for him; barley.

We were both wearing Indian band-aids over our eyebrows. Nickel Eye's rose together in the middle just slightly. They made him look sad.

'Don't,' I said, but he did anyway, led me deeper into the Plains, the grass folding in behind us. I don't know what emotion my eyebrows were locked in: fear, pity, respect. My hand was small in his. I was an agent of the law; he was the first documented Indian serial-killer. It was a dance, a spotlight dance, and I closed my eyes in it, for it, opened them to the sun, not harsh but nurturing. A Pueblo kind of heat, from my childhood. And there was that same wonder: we were standing in a field of hair—Indian hair. Growing in clumps from the ground like the grass they plant in fallow fields; recovery grass.

I could feel my band-aids now. They were trying to close my eyes, deny all this. How the wind lifted the blue-black hair, how it rustled.

'Are there...*people* under there?' I asked, my hand over my mouth, and Nickel Eye just said *America, America*, in a way that drove me from my sheets night after night, from my room at The Broken Arrow (219b), a weekly place of neon and moths and vending machines. Fool's Hip squatted dark in the distance, blotting out the lowest stars.

'No,' I said, coughing tar, pushing whatever button was brightest, promising to eat whatever dropped. When I went back in the morning—in daylight—the brightest button was either potato chips or licorice, but I remembered neither. All that remained was the walk back, past the TV lounge, Cat Stand there in the pale glow, her back to the world, the vanilla ice cream collected at the corners of her mouth, her right arm shivering cold, even under all that flannel.

'I know you,' I said, and she just looked away, and I ate whatever was in my hand, and, before I left, touched my eyebrows. But my fingertips were numb. Maybe it was chocolate—the machine had given me chocolate. It kept me up all night, anyway. She was my first interview.

The American didn't make it out alive, either, like I thought. Number forty. It must have happened when I was with Denim Horse those two days, saying his name over and over. Here's how I picture it: the American gets off the bus for the second time, back for Mary Boy's tattoo. It has something he needs. He's lighter now, drawn up around the ribs, no longer eating right. This time he dabs Jesus' face with a cocktail napkin, pockets the dark blood, then shuffles around Fool's Hip until Nickel Eye settles on him— his sandy, receding hair, his citizen dress. The crisp bills he's been trading for beer.

He doesn't get any drunker, though, the American—any easier—and that's when I lose him to the exit doors, rattling as the bus pulls away. He walks out after it just for the gesture, so he can tell his wife and kids that this is the way it happened. Maybe this is the way it's always been happening.

When he turns back to Fool's Hip, the coyote is there, ears back, lips flat. They lock eyes, one of them grins, and then they're moving, the coyote padding out into the grassland, looking back to make sure the American is following, that he wants it this way too. His name was Enil Anderson, remember? This was when I called the station from the payphone at Broken Arrow, traded my badge number for an address. Enil's address. His old one. His house with the garage.

It was still there, in a row with the rest. There were two families living in and around it, but I told them to leave. They did. I walked through the house as he might have, then, cataloging furniture positions, hearing children's voices from walls; holding onto the banister a little too long. Number forty. All the names rose in the back of my throat—Janie, Luis, Kathleen; Philip, Mark, Amy. And now Enil. Maybe even forty-one: back at Fool's Hip, through a haze of smoke, I looked down the alley and asked Back Iron about Owen82.

He settled his outlined eyes on me. Today he was wearing the wide, black frames of a pair of glasses, the lenses somewhere else. 'You part of the task force?' he asked, and his voice stayed there at the top of the question, time dilating around the two of us; blooming. A custom-ball rolled end over end down the lane, exhaling smoke from its thumbhole with every individual revolution. Like a little train, an iron horse leaving curlicues of ash, perfect little whorls, identification, God.

When I looked from the ball back to Back Iron I didn't say anything, couldn't. And he was smiling. 'His investigation,' he finished, directing me to LP Deal, the heel of his hand against his upper lip, shiny with saliva.

'He's the one that found him,' I repeated, from the report. My voice though, it was hardly me anymore. All the pins in the place crashed into each other at once.

'No shit he found him,' Back Iron said, winking. 'Gutshot, you know?'

I nodded, drew my pistol-finger casual against my side. Back Iron moved it around to the front, a difficult angle.

'And it was cold,' he said, and then explained the stainless-steel thumbjoint Owen82 had inherited from his grandmother, who had gotten it from her father. He held the large joint of his thumb up to show, and I became aware of my own in a new way—trying to hold a pistol perpendicular to my navel, the metal and plastic stiff in my hand from the weather, my breath visible, measured.

'How long did it take him?'

'To die?'

'Like that.' My gun-hand was still there.

Now Back Iron shrugged, pushed his hair out of his face, in sync with LP, halfway across Fool's Hip, and seemed to look over his shoulder at the bathrooms, across the lockers, to the bar. To Nickel Eye. 'Hour,' he said, suddenly sick with it. 'Maybe two.' And then he looked directly at me through the frames of his glasses: 'You should know, though,' he said, just low enough for me to doubt. But I couldn't.

Back Iron was already laughing with his eyes, leaning back; letting me off. I ran to Denim Horse that night, pulled his hair to be sure it was him, and then said his name over and over, trying to drown out the sound of Back Iron somewhere past the bedroom window, dribbling his basketball evenly into a pad of concrete, my dress whipping around his knees.

RED DAWN. It was the name of the video game Naitche and LP went back and forth on, trading high-scores. The first stage was 'Gunfight at the Mediocre Corral.' The last was 'Red Rover, Red Rover.' The status-panel was North America, going red from Mexico on up. Either there was no sound or LP had turned it off somehow. They concentrated so hard on it I could hear the blood pulsing in their temples, washing up out of the pit the arcade was, into Fool's Hip proper. It was beautiful. They were like father and son but not, more like brothers, like LP was just an older version of Naitche. An older, flawed version. When they were hunched over the game together, though—or even when it was just Naitche, LP on mop-duty—the rest of the video games were mute, their heads down in respect, or fear. The clan bowlers were the same way with his mother—standing back, unsure—but Cat Stand didn't care.

'She doesn't know,' Eddie Dial said, watching her bowl.

I waited for more.

'That she's supposed to lose when they come.'

The Councilmen. The AllSkin tournament. Courtney Peltdowne had been taping flyers up on the glass doors all morning. Her lips had been lined with cowdrops, her hands moving in slow motion with the clear tape, but Mary Boy wouldn't take it away from her. I didn't realize she was taller than me until I stood beside her, reading her handiwork.

'Deersoft Bird,' she was saying, 'Plumy Deer Bird,' and more.

I shook my head no, and she laughed a little.

'Not you, girl,' her *grand*mother; she was trying to reconstruct her grandmother's name from her own—*Peltdowne*. The corruption.

'I can *feel* it,' she said, the name, her name. When she smiled there was a cowdrop halogen white between her teeth.

'So are you really Indian?' she asked, and then—her eyes on Denim Horse the whole time—leaned forward and kissed me on the lips, the pill passing between us. It was already warm, slick.

Yes, I nodded, her hand in my synthetic hair. *Yes yes yes.*

In the bathroom with her that afternoon, our reflections smearing from stall to stall, she led me to the corner. It was decaying, cracking. She rolled her sleeve up, closed her eyes to make her fingers work better, and eased her arm through the cinderblock, birthed a stack of notebooks.

'What is it?' I asked.

'Thirty-two B,' she said.

That was the first time I saw LP's manifesto—his tight, cramped hand, the uneven lines; the fever.

'Read it to me,' I said, and for a while she did.

| Indian Corn

1854

They were probably Sioux. It was the right area, at least: South Dakota, before there was a South Dakota. Fourteen of them, splintered off from their tiospaye, sulking through the grasslands after meat. Of the four horses, two were lashed to travois. The other two ranged ahead, one to the north, one the south, their riders sweated to their backs; content. ¶ Three nights ago they'd come across a covered wagon. They used it to patch their lodges. The patches were harsh white against the smoke-blackened leather, curling up at the edges like the scabs they knew. It was medicine of some kind, anyway. The dogs could tell, and that was enough. ¶ Five days from the wagon they found half a copper breastplate dull in the sun, and Horns In Back looked at it only once and told them a long story about a turtle shell, his hands moving over each syllable until his words were shiny and worn and sacred. The next morning Maddy Bride cooked two rabbits in the breast-plate, and all that day Runs To The Tree and Billy made circles around camp, dragging wood in. It burned hot enough and long enough to make arrow points from the breast-plate, and Horns In Back was singing anyway, so it had to work. ¶This was the winter marked with the yellow arrow. No children were born, but no one died either. They were fourteen strong. Their horses had the man from the wagon's buttons braided into their bridles. When the man had seen Billy with his two carbines, the stocks decorated with tacks, he had let the traces go, then clubbed his wife to death. Billy had smiled: for two weeks he wore strips of the wife's dress around his calves, but then the fabric got stiff and loud. ¶The man he had killed the same way he killed the rabbits for stew. ¶Two weeks from the turtle shell, the sky to the north was black with birds, and they knew what it meant: raw, skinless humps of buffalo, no good to eat. Horns In Back made them ride until the smell was gone. The next day he started the ceremony for the Freak Pipe. It took four days to completely unwrap and four more days to light. He sang careful songs. Runs To The Tree and Billy had to ride out farther and farther each day for meat, but each day they found it. Maddy Bride said this was good: it meant the Freak Pipe wanted them to stay here for the ceremony. Her two sons had never seen it, either, hadn't been born the last time. It was only done every few years. Only Horns In Back knew it anymore. That night he told them the story of it, the pink stone the pipe was carved from, the generations that had put their lips to it, looked down along its length and back to themselves. Billy made drum noises with his mouth because they didn't have one, and his voice filled the night until his main wife Gauche screamed and Runs To The Tree tilted his bow straight up, slung one of their yellow-tipped arrows against the blackness, trying to pierce it. ¶It came back down into the flank of one of their decorated horses, but the horse didn't run. In the morning Maddy Bride's youngest son would point to an out-of-place bird balanced on the worn nock, picking at the fletching, and after that they would call the boy Bird. No one would ever ride that horse again, though. ¶But first there was the ceremony. Horns In Back rubbed paint onto his face with a rag, then painted his fingertips from his cheeks, because everything had to be backwards. So night was morning, in was out, the smoke flaps were closed until everyone's eyes bled, even the children, unable to blink. ¶'Look away,' Horns In Back said, however you say it in Sioux, and nobody did.

1855

The year marked with striped grass, purple lines of it feeling out across the prairie like blood poisoning. Because Horns In Back wouldn't let them cross any of them, the lines—and the horses wouldn't anyway—they rode west to go north, and brushed the grass in place behind them because they weren't alone. There were balls of light in the distance some nights, the small voices of a camp. ¶Horns In Back stood long one night trying to pick it out from the low-lying stars, but the stars were even wrong, and he told Billy and Maddy Bride and Runs To The Tree and Stands Twice to watch his hands until morning, see if he was still holding the Freak Pipe. All of them forgot except Bird, though, and he was hiding behind a rack of drying meat, watching the canvas patches on the lodge. They framed Horns In Back like eyes, looking deeper than he could. ¶A dog barked and soon they all were, and the horse with the arrow shaft healed into its flank trotted behind the dogs, one of them now. The short robe who had followed them with his two sticks ('†') had named it Judas for the way it held its head, but when the name hadn't stuck, Stands Twice took it for himself. It was power: Judas Horse. ¶They waved to the short robe when he left walking, and smiled like he would live forever, even though they knew he was riding into Crow land. Let them steal his wooden beads. What Horns In Back's band needed was greased bullets for their guns. This was the winter Maddy Bride's oldest son died coughing, and she left her hair on top of the grass for the birds, but then Bird took it because it was his brother—it *had been* his brother. He braided it with tail hair from the dog horse, for medicine, and wore it around his neck, tight as a choker. ¶Later that night they all saw it, and knew it was a sign: a yellow square flashing two hills over—once, twice, smaller and smaller until it was gone. Bird held his choker between his thumb and index finger and hummed, and Maddy Bride pulled him close, looked out there for Runs To The Tree and Judas Horse and Billy. They all looked at each other, then to Horns In Back, who nodded. ¶They were gone until dawn, and when they came back wouldn't talk, just started collecting the slender branches of a sweat. Before they ducked in, though, Billy stood for a long time at the entrance to Maddy Bride's lodge. He was watching Bird. 'I'm not him,' Bird said, finally, and Billy nodded, and Maddy Bride looked eight days behind them, where her oldest son was buried, and nodded too.

1857

Winter had left them thin and parched. Runs To The Tree had gone hunting, shot once, then never returned. Horns In Back nodded as if everything was as it was supposed to be, and then no one said Runs To The Tree's name again, ever, even when they found him in the coulee, a small hole in one side of his grinning skull, a larger hole in the other side. He was already in the forks of a tree so they left him there with a twist of tobacco and one of the yellow arrows and the dog horse. The dog horse didn't stay with him though; Billy still saw it in the trees or between the rocks, its black hooves wrapped in the soft skin of a calf so it made no noise. Horns In Back watched his hands all the time now. Maddy Bride watched him watch his hands, held Bird close. ¶'What is it?' Judas Horse asked, not looking directly at her, but she wouldn't tell him, so he wrapped his own feet in the soft skin of a calf, moved silent from tree to tree, taking the velvety deer any way he wanted, walking back into camp with them slung over his shoulder. No one would eat them though, not even the porcupine who rolled into camp disguised as a dry weed. 'It's nothing,' Horns In Back said, but it was. The porcupine laughed four times as it rolled away, leaving no quills for roaches or plumes. Maddy Bride kept two pouches of pemmican tied just above her hips, inside her clothes, just in case. At first the dogs could smell it, but soon they left her alone. ¶ Three days from the porcupine, the dog horse skylined itself on a ridge for them, and its silhouette opened up into button-sized holes, little suns in its side. Billy felt one of the greased shooters thump into the grass at his feet. As the sound rolled in he crouched, never looking away from the dog horse, and dug the slug from the ground. It was still hot. He handed it to Horns In Back and Horns In Back put it hissing to his tongue, looked to the dog horse, still not falling, even when the shooters walked up beside it with their long guns and their boots, silver at the toes and heels. When Maddy Bride looked down to Bird, Bird was holding the Freak Pipe. He had unwrapped it too fast. She wailed, but there was nothing to do; they had to smoke it, go deeper into this still. ¶ As Horns In Back led them to a spot, Billy looked back once to the ridge, the white men touching the dog horse with the tips of their guns, and when he turned back, Horns In Back was walking in front of Judas Horse's horse, and for a moment Billy saw Horns In Back through Judas Horse's calf: it was a perfect, fifty-caliber hole, bloodless. He had never smoked the Freak Pipe twice this close together. Nobody had. He sung his power song to himself and followed.

1860

Bird was growing up, going out with Billy to hunt when Maddy Bride let him, and even when she didn't. The name he chose when it was time was 'Bird,' just like his old one. Horns In Back said not to do it like that, but he had already done it. ¶ For giveaway he gave to Horns In Back three horses he had led away from a soldier camp. They were good horses; Horns In Back nodded once, held his robe together at the neck. ¶ Once just after the snow they rode up on the buffalo humps, skinned, still steaming, the air still ringing, smelling hot, and Maddy Bride walked to the top of the hill, looked east on the chance that this was the same herd they had smelled six winters ago and skirted. She couldn't tell, but when she looked back down, one of the cows stood, tongueless, skinned, and Judas Horse fell on it. He wore a white head-on ermine skin around the hole in his calf. The cow died under his knife, and they took her intestine where it was thick, turned it inside out then stuffed it with fat, tied it at both ends, ate it until their chins dripped grease and they weren't afraid of anything. But they were. Judas Horse wouldn't eat it, wouldn't eat at all. He would die in four moons, his bones pushing through his skin, and after he died the hole in his calf would finally bleed out so Horns In Back could sing over him. ¶ They were down to eleven now, then ten when Gauche's younger sister cut her hand on a square nail in a lodgepole from when it had been a tree. It was just a scratch. At the fire after she died, Bird asked Maddy Bride if she remembered the yellow arrows, and she said she remembered that one, anyway, she remembered how that dog horse had saved all their lives. Maybe it was still standing, even. ¶Bird smiled, stirred the coals. That night he ate the pemmican his mother had kept tied to her side for three years. Behind him the canvas patches of the lodge stared out across the grassland, at the voices that never went away anymore. Some of the dogs that had been born since the Freak Pipe didn't know what the night was like without those voices, Billy said, then traded two of them to another band for a beaded parfleche. When they saw that band again just before winter, the woman who had beaded the parfleche was wearing a blanket from the fort and staring at him the whole time. He tried to give the case back, but she didn't want it, wanted her son instead, her brother, who had eaten the dogs. ¶Horns In Back led his people away, and didn't stop riding for six days, and then it was just to stand in the middle of floodwater, his horse's tail whipping the surface, fish nipping at it. ¶Watching them, Bird finally threw up his mother's pemmican. It swirled in the current and eddied away, and in the time it took for Bird to wipe the back of his mouth, Horns In Back had fallen from his cavalry saddle, was underwater nipping at hairs in the sunlight as well, having his vision, the one they used to mark the year: it started there at the flood, the ten of them all turned towards the sun, but then the sun halved itself and halved itself again, lined the sky like the wooden beads of the short robe who had to be dead by now. ¶'Look away,' the short robe said, pointing up with one finger so Horns In Back could see the back of his hand, the veins blue there, and because the Freak Pipe was still unwrapped, Horns In Back looked harder, beneath the black robes, to the breastplate beneath, lined like a turtle shell. 'Look,' the turtle said in a voice Horns In Back knew, and before Horns In Back could remember to do the opposite, it was too late he'd already followed the pointed finger through the hole in Judas Horse's calf to a white buffalo calf standing two rises over, calling for its mother then turning to Horns In Back, nosing through the grass towards him, rising to walk on two legs like a child, yellow and blue and red thunderbolts standing in the ground at all four corners of the sky, which was the back of the short-robe's hand, Judas Horse's ermine skin raising its head, opening its mouth to receive this white thing the hand was holding, and that was when Billy pulled Horns In Back from the flood. ¶That night they rode to the highest ground they could find and waited for Horns In Back to tell all this to them, and when it was over, Bird arranged the choker of his brother's hair on the stones by the fire. In the morning it was gone, and that's how he knew they were alone, it was just them now. With the first snowfall he followed Billy out for meat day after day, and it was always there for them, and it tasted like it always had, but it was different, too.

1861

The year of the cat. It just started following them. Gauche said it was from the fort they'd passed four days before, always keeping it on the right, but Horns In Back had been seeing it before then, even, when it was still bellydown at the edge of the light, the dogs whimpering. Earlier that day they'd found three men under a tree. One of them was hung from a rope, but they were all dead. Billy took one of their hats and Bird matched two pair of boots from the two on the ground, but then left them a few hours later when they filled with seed from the tall grass. ¶ The cat went in and out of the lodges. No one talked around it. For voices it had to go to the other camp, out past where they could see. Sometimes it stayed there for days, then came back fat. Once it returned heavy with kittens, but they were all stillborn, and not even Horns In Back would skin them to line his moccasins. ¶ He wasn't watching his hands anymore, but they could all see it by now, the fluted pink stone, worn by generations, scorched at the end he always kept closest to the ground. It would take more than four days to wrap it now; it would take the rest of his life. But Horns In Back never looked at it anymore, kept his eyes on the horizon instead, not for the voices or the cat slinking back, but for the white buffalo calf that was supposed to lead them back to the real land, with the real meat and the real grass. ¶ When Gauche had her second child, they could see through the skin of its hands for twelve days, until Maddy Bride was holding it one night, standing on the shadow side of the lodge, and one of its small hands passed before her face. Through it she saw the other camp, or the shape of it, blotting out the stars like a short mesa, steam rising all around it. She handed the child back to Gauche and never held it again, but Horns In Back watched her all that next morning and knew. ¶ Three days later they found one of their yellow arrows rotting in the grass and Billy calmly got down from his horse and buried it. No one said anything; they were riding in circles, in cycles, on top of themselves. Soon Bird would go out for wood and Runs To The Tree would be there, the cat rubbing against his sunbleached shinbone. ¶ Once Maddy Bride tied a piece of ribbon from a dead girl they'd found to the cat, and it was gone for days, came back with a different ribbon, maybe from another dead girl, maybe the same one. ¶ Horns In Back sang songs so the white calf could hear them, and Bird sang them in his head as he followed Billy from ridge to ridge. They both carried lances now, with scalps or feathers or skins or whatever tied near the head, swaying in the wind as they sat horseback, staring off into the night. They were too close to each other to be able to see, and no one would tell them that their silhouettes were like the dog horse's had been that day: pocked with light. But they hadn't been shot. If Maddy Bride had looked at them from the back, it would have been like with Gauche's child all over, and she would have pounded berries into meat and tied it all over her body, until the birds came and carried her away, back.

1861, again

Gauche's child was dead. Horns In Back had sung over it and they had buried it like white people then walked backwards away from it for two days, even the horses and the dogs.

Two moons later Horns In Back had his second vision, and in this one he was young and marching, being marched by the cavalry, and he heard one of the old men beside him say 'There it is,' and it was a wide black bird riding the column of heat all their bodies were, and the old man kept his eyes fixed on it the whole march, until the soldiers greased their round gun up and made Horns In Back and his band stand shoulder to shoulder. The bird never left, even when the gun filled the daylight with smoke, and the old man who had been watching it was the first to die. ¶ In the sweat lodge Billy and Bird built for Horns In Back to understand this, Horns In Back said that the old man asked him what kind of bird it was, right before he died, and Horns In Back hadn't been able to tell. Billy curled his lip and looked away, not believing. Bird either. Even though it was Horns In Back. After that they left his meat in front of his old patched lodge without calling out, so that by the time he got out there he had to beat the dogs off. Maddy Bride said none of this was right, and Gauche nodded, nodded. Gauche's oldest, born just before the Year of the Yellow Arrows, was running everywhere now, learning to talk. Like the younger dogs, he didn't know what the night was like without the murmur of voices; he would be scared of the silence if they ever made it back from here. ¶ Three camps over, her oldest came to her to ask her about the horse with the soft feet. He had seen it in the trees, watching them with human eyes. Gauche left camp that next morning and never came back. The whole tiospaye could fit in one lodge now. A day's ride away, Bird found a doe crushed, her eyes still open, her legs at all the wrong angles. He looked up to see where she could have fallen from, but there was nothing. All around. Just the grassland. He quartered her and left a piece of her in front of Horns In Back's lodge, but Horns In Back wouldn't eat it. ¶ They hadn't seen anyone for eighteen moons now, since the dead men at the tree, though once two horses wandered into camp, both mares. They were wearing saddles inlaid with silver, the horns reaching up to the middle of Billy's stomach. Maddy Bride used a bone file to rub them off for Billy and Bird—the horns—but all she could do with the back of the saddle was rub notches in it. Billy and Bird used them until the second snow, when they had to burn them for warmth. The smoke they made was thick and sweet, and it was like the old times, when they would find a wagon and take it apart, try to put it together into something else, something they could use.

1863
The year Bird died and Maddy Bride left her hair on the grass again. He was the fifth skin to die since the Freak Pipe. When Maddy Bride said it like that—spit it—Horns In Back said listen, and told them that he knew where they were now: on a tanned elk skin he'd seen once years ago, when it fell off someone's pack. It was the story of The Fifth Skin, only he was seeing it, not hearing it, and what he was seeing was four people dead and then a fifth dying too, but coming back. The four who died first pushed the fifth back, up. ¶ Bird had

died like Runs To The Tree had died, though: with a small hole in one side of his head, a larger one on the other side; shot. Maddy Bride said she didn't want him to come back. ¶ In the days after they left Bird in his tree, Billy ranged farther and farther out for meat, and always found it. He didn't tell anyone, but the wide black bird from Horns In Back's second vision had been showing him where the meat was, and once he had seen his son moving through the tall grass after him. His son was almost transparent now, but his hair was slick with grease, so he was finding meat too, somewhere. He didn't say his name, though, but rode away, because soon Gauche would rise from the grass too, running after her son, and he knew he would follow if he saw her, that the camp would starve. But maybe that would be best, too: eating the wrong-meat was making them wrong as well. ¶ That night Billy called out when he dropped Horns In Back's meat off, and stood there guarding it until Horns In Back leaned up from his flap. ¶ 'Where is he?' Billy asked, looking away, wherever the two eyes on Horns In Back's lodge were looking, and Horns In Back bunched his shoulders together in imitation of whatever Bird was going through and it was like he was in his mother again, fists up near his face. ¶ That night Billy said Bird's name where Maddy Bride could hear it, even if she pretended not to, and the next day when they were riding, the ground beneath them got louder, harder, even though it was just grass, and one of the new mares began running, her shod hooves leaving sparks that set the land on fire. Horns In Back's band ran from it until the lodge poles they were using for the travois were worn to nubs, and then they stood facing it, waiting, and it passed, taking all their breath with it, scorching their leggings and their eyelashes but that was all. It was the Year of the Black Moccasins. Everything burned. The black ash collected in the corners and rims of their eyes and around their lips until they were painted like clowns, but not holy, just lost. And still the other camp remained, still Billy sat his horse at dusk, the butt of his lance pushing a shiny spot in the ground, whatever was hanging off it swaying in the wind. He didn't smile. Sometimes now Horns In Back joined him, the Freak Pipe left alone in his lodge, on a spit carved from shed antlers. It was still smoking, and Horns In Back didn't have to say to Billy that maybe *they* were still smoking it that first time, that maybe Bird was still young, Gauche still back at camp rubbing brains into skin, Judas Horse still using his first name. ¶ Billy had been the one to find Bird, though. The crumbling bank beside him was splattered red, and Bird was still warm, and the gun he had found was still in his hand, Bird's. Billy had buried it, arranged Bird, then taken Bird's pouch from around his neck, weighed the yellow arrowhead in it then slung it up as high as he could. It never came down.

186x

The last recorded year. When Billy saw something coming to them from the other camp and gripped his lance tighter, finally raised it for the camp to see, to come see. Maddy

Bride was the first to make it up the rise, Horns In Back the last. Behind them meat sizzled and boiled and horses stamped and blew and a lodgeflap opened and closed, breathing smoke out. The grassland was greener than it had ever been that year, from the fire. The dogs were fat from rabbits and moles. Three days ago Billy had walked the horses single file through a prairie-dog town so wide they had to camp twice to get across it. Horns In Back had left small pieces of chewed meat at the edge of the light for the prairie-dog people. But they didn't mark the year with the prairie-dog people walking into camp, inspecting all their goods, taking all the brass buttons to trade underground. ¶ The voices were louder now, too, and Sioux, but not Sioux. Maybe Horns In Back's tiospaye had been gone long enough that the people had changed. They would still expect him to have the Freak Pipe, though, but he had left it smoking on its antler spit many moons ago. There was no wrapping for it anymore, no bundle. He watched it as they left, too, and saw what happened: an impossibly tall wasichu in citizen dress had rolled over the opposite hill, blinking in the Dakota sun, the Freak Pipe drawing him in. Once there he knelt, danced around it, knelt again, squinted at the sun and unfolded a piece of paper from his jacket, rolled it into a cigarette with no tobacco—with words for tobacco—and inserted it into the Pipe, settled it back into its spit, and loped off. Horns In Back couldn't see through him like he could everybody else; the tall man was solid, black. ¶ When Billy doubled back to bring Horns In Back along, he didn't see the tall man running away, but the shadow of his wide bird racing up the hill. ¶ 'Should we wrap it?' Billy asked, about the pipe, and Horns In Back lifted his fingers to the sky all around, meaning it was. It's just that they were in with it now. Neither of them looked back again, just forward, through the prairie-dog town, to the next camp and the next, and the next. ¶ Sometimes Billy still found Maddy Bride's hair woven into the top of the grass in mourning, and he kept it, stranded it all together into a breastplate spaced with rifle brass. He would never wear it, though. It was too powerful, too light. It was for his son, or for Bird or for Judas Horse, to protect them from the yellow arrow still falling out of the sky one day. They would have to be lying on their back, though. Billy was thinking about this when he saw it, gripped his lance: it was a puff of white far out in the grassland, as far as he could see, but slowly it stumbled forward into the shape of a buffalo calf, and he raised his lance, laughed, and when Maddy Bride saw it she laughed too, and they were all laughing, for the first time in years.

Skin Deep

PINK EYE was all the rage. You could get it in the community center swimming pools, from eye-liner pencils, at the right taco stands,
supposedly from buffalo. It was the STD of choice, even. Denim
Horse's eyes bled with it. He even gave it to a tourist who didn't
know she was Indian until him, came to Fool's Hip that next
morning with her sandy hair in braids. Courtney Peltdowne stood
in the fan of the ball return, ashing calmly into the thumbholes.
She didn't smile back at the Indian tourist, or at the knowledge of
me in Denim Horse's trailer, saying his name in every language I
knew—English—trying to get around the vaccine the department
required. It was never enough, though. The vaccine was the only

thing IHS had ever done right. But there are ways. There are always ways.

When I could feel the cowdrops drying my contacts out, I followed my fingertips along the carpet of the back wall until the pit yawned before me. LP Deal and Naitche were crowded at the console of Red Dawn, their eyes straining, teeth set, leaning into it. The backside of my face spread into a smile; I placed my quarters on the glass, in line. LP Deal and Naitche never looked up.

That first day I learned the controls over their shoulders. By the second day my fingertips were blistered from the cue ball set into the deck of the game; your initials were all over it, Blue Plume. By the third day I was stepping up out of the pit like LP Deal did, like Naitche did, as a deer would, ready to flit away with the least sound. I was insubstantial; my eyes were so bloodshot. Twice Back Iron stood on the lip of the pit, watching me; twice he walked away. Once I lowered my head to talk down my sleeve but caught myself at the last instant, looked up at LP Deal.

'It's okay,' he said, but it wasn't, I couldn't, so he offered me his wrist. I took his hand in both of mine, my thumbs on either side of his upturned palm, and five hundred years fell away, two thousand, more.

LP Deal was touching my hair now.

'Who are you?' I asked.

'He doesn't know.'

I turned, caught. It was Mary Boy. Behind his permanent sunglasses his eyes were any color. He stared LP Deal back to his broom, let Naitche fade back into the hum and glow of the arcade. Behind me was Red Dawn, and from its quarter slot there was a braided line of sinew, nervous like the tail of a mouse.

'You're looking for her, right?' he asked.

Special Agent Chassis Jones.

I managed a half-smile. 'Maybe.'

'All by yourself?'

I nodded.

'And you think she's down here?' he asked, rolling a plug of tobacco across his stubby tongue, mocking me, leaning over to look under a pinball machine, giving me his left side, his left shoulder. It was intentional; I braced myself for his partial Jesus like I'd learned to, the way you brace yourself for a ruler across the back of your hand, but then Mary Boy's shoulder was bare, clean. All the water in my body rushed hot to the back of my eyes. It was a miracle: there was no ink, no face, no Oklahoma; no christ. Behind me the mouse tail of sinew twitched and whipped inward, disappearing into the slot, the quarter scurrying deeper, nosing into the pool of change, hiding.

Mary Boy came back from the pinball machine with a coyote grin. Or whoever he was. 'What?' he asked, massaging his naked shoulder, your initials scrolling down all around us.

I shook my head no, nothing, it was nothing, but then he was stepping closer, removing his glasses one lens at a time.

Nickel Eye.

His lips were black and dry and sharp at the corners. He tipped the faded bowler he wasn't wearing and my eyes brimmed with tears I didn't have and I closed them—accepting his gesture—and then he drew closer still, cradling the base of my skull between the wide thumb and forefinger of his left hand and pushing the thumb and forefinger of his other hand past my lips, around my teeth like a mouthpiece, back to where my tongue started. Where Courtney Peltdowne had lined the cowdrops for me in the bathroom three days ago. He scraped them out one by one and gave them to me like pearls, closing my hand around them. He was wearing his BDU jacket again, like a veteran. The back was threadbare from leaning over his beer. Already Fool's Hip was coming together again into hard edges and angles, the milk leaving my eyes, draining down the back of my throat.

I would be sick from it later, but now, now: Nickel Eye.

He was waiting for me to say thank you.

Instead I pushed him away, my thumbnails clicking together on the follow-through.

'Where did you put him?' I asked.

He caught himself on the lip of the pinball machine, winked. 'I thought it was a her...?'

'*Enil Anderson.*'

'Oh,' Nickel Eye said, feigning a hundred different things in the space of a shrug, the pinball paddles applauding his retreat, '*him*,' then said maybe he just went home, yeah?

No.

But still.

I got Eddie Dial to call for me that afternoon. It was all real casual, very Navajo. While we were waiting for the callback, I told him I knew what Indian Corn tasted like.

'More like American cheese,' he said back—LP Deal's manifesto—and then the phone was a white ringing thing and I was lounging in its general direction, trading Special Agent Chassis Jones' badge number for an address again, this one in America. I wrote it on a napkin and stared at it until the numbers swam. I was crying.

Eddie Dial led me back to the table.

'You know that Fifth Skin's a joke,' he said, 'right?' then showed me, licked the edges of my address napkin and tore them away from the miniature shape of a cured elk hide. I could almost smell the urine and brains rising from it. He held his finger up for me to wait, though, wait, then massaged a pencil from his shirt pocket, drew it all out for me like a wintercount: the yellow arrow, the Judas horse. Gauche scurrying off into the grass.

'He's just translating,' Eddie Dial said, boring a period into the napkin after *186x.*

'Are you sure?'

He nodded.

'Then what? He's translating what?'

'You know.'

And I did: nestled under my tongue in the abscess burned by the cowdrops was a soapstone figurine of Courtney Peltdowne in a shawl that wasn't a shawl, was an old wintercount she'd pulled from the hand dryer somehow, where it backed up to the wall the lockers were on. She spread her arms like a moth, rising, rising.

I threw up in the ashtray.

'It's not easy, those things,' Eddie Dial said. They were still in my hand. I could start it all over if I wanted. Nickel Eye was watching me through the glass bottom of his mug, though. LP Deal too, through the dreadlock strands of his mop, Back Iron through his reckless mascara, Denim Horse through his unbraided hair, Mary Boy from his crouched place behind the pins, his opera glasses glinting, Cat Stand's sixteen-pound ball hurtling down the lane at him, each revolution leaving a fine pawprint of ash.

I opened my hand and the cowdrops were flat white, like milk, like beads of milk. I poured all but one of them into LP Deal's mop bucket. They hissed in the grey water. The last one I took to the bathroom because it was evidence, but then had it back in my mouth by the time the door closed.

The capillaries in the white part of my eyes bloomed, aching with pleasure. It was like the game—the redness washing up me, over me.

'You alright?' a voice asked—female, not mine—and I didn't open my eyes, just nodded, said that sometimes blood gets in my eyes, that's all. It was funny; she laughed, came into focus: the Indian tourist, sitting on the sink, braiding her hair by touch, her back to the mirror, lip bitten with effort. The braid was perfect. I smiled around Nickel Eye's thick fingers still in my mouth, and then flinched from Cat Stand's ball, crashing into the pins of Lane 8, spreading them all over Fool's Hip.

On the stall someone had written *roses are red*, only scratched out the *roses*-part.

'My new name is Miss America,' the Indian tourist said, looking down, peeking up. ~~Fresh~~ Exhausted from whatever naming ceremony Denim Horse had made up. 'Is that good...*Indian*?'

'What was your old one?' I asked, crossing to the hand dryer.

'Dorita,' she said. 'Like the chip. Dorita Dawes.'

'Dorita,' I repeated, staring hard at the hand dryer, at nothing else but the dryer, 'watch this,' and pushed my arm as deep into the wall as I could.

That night at the Broken Arrow, Cat Stand looked up at me from the television set. From Dairyland; America. For thirty seconds she was twelve years old again, and I smiled at her, but she didn't smile back, just turned her head off-screen. I moved to the door to get a better angle into the set, to see what she was seeing, and it was me, standing at the edge of the parking lot, looking out. And I was. The gravel and shattered glass crunched under my bare feet, and then didn't stop when I did.

Something was out there with me; someone.

I breathed, breathed, and for a moment she was there, hunched over, scurrying: Gauche.

'Hello,' I said.

Behind me a horse snorted and I turned to it, followed it to what Broken Arrow used to be: a one-room schoolhouse built the same distance away from all the bands. Where Gauche had to have been scurrying to. It was maybe 1907. Cat Stand was already there, still twelve. Courtney Peltdowne too, staring holes in me, and Back Iron and Denim Horse and LP Deal. LP Deal was Naitche, though. And he was wearing my contacts. I sat down beside him, and together we watched the Great Plains Fire guttering out across the prairie, trailing a plume of ash miles deep. It was serene, all of us as children, our hair in swept piles on the floor, our canvas shoes sizes too large, the annotated Code open on our desks, Gauche at the front of the classroom, explaining Bacteen in academic terms, how in all emergence tales—whether ex nihlo or ex-America—the supernatural is facilitated by a comical social misfit with extraordinary abilities, a trickster figure who reinforces current social mores, and on and on until Bacteen became Nickel Eye for me and the blood thrushing in my ears ordered itself into discrete blocks of sound, into a hesitant knock on the door, my door; 219b.

I stood before it for long moments, sure it was Gauche, sure it wasn't, but when I finally opened it, it was Naitche, only I called him LP and he ran away, breathing through his nose.

The sound missing from the night was a basketball.

I closed the door gently, with both hands—one on the knob, pulling, the other just above it, pushing—then watched the late movie first with no sound, then with no color, then with no electricity, by memory. The last cowdrop was hours old already. When it was gone my stomach clutched after it. In the bathroom mirror I held my pistol finger to each of my eyes in turn, left my contacts on the edge of the sink; blinked.

The bathroom was so white without them. I could hear the pipes now, too. They all led to the toilet. I shook my head no, no: in that desperate part at the back of the bowl, just above the throat where you have to stare, was a set of numbers. A phone number. The Aborigine Hotline. I said no out loud, held my hair out of the water, turned myself inside out.

It didn't help: two hours later I was on the phone with them.

It was like walking into a pawnshop; within four minutes I was bargaining for the cassette I'd pulled from the hand dryer, giving them a sample, a taste.

'Who is it?' they asked, my middle finger on the pause button.

'I don't know,' I said, and then played the rest, LP Deal mumbling into his wrist about his mother, fading into the noise of a pandance, pulling his ear to the ground to listen for her return.

'It was like his head was heavy, then,' the hotline anthropologist said, and then the line went dead, some telegraph pole out in the grassland falling into firewood or travois runner, and in the silence I heard it again, a scurrying, only this time it was in the receiver: someone was listening.

'Hello?' I said, barely giving it any voice this time, and a single, frosted breath drifted from the mouthpiece—ice cream—and I was back in the schoolhouse with Cat Stand, only now a white child was there, his wrists under the table tied, his fingernails throbbing blue. He was listening to Gauche with the rest of us; she wasn't talking about a massacre, but the days before the massacre, when her band was being marched away from the fort, how one of the old men told her that as long as she watched the eagle in front of them, nothing bad could happen.

'Don't look away,' he said, in Cree, Creek, Crow, something, 'it matters that he's there, an eagle like that,' bald or golden, whatever's good, but she did look away, to watch him, the old man, see if he was watching too. He was. And he never looked down, even when the Gatling gun started its whining spin. He was the first to die.

'But—' LP Deal started to say, but he was Naitche, mute. Cat Stand clapped a hand over his mouth to remind him, and Denim Horse clapped a hand over her mouth, and Back Iron over Denim Horse, around the whole classroom until Courtney Peltdowne's hand was rushing towards my face, a cowdrop neatly palmed.

I pursed my lips just in time.

It was maybe 1907.

Back Iron took me to America when I asked. He had a skirt wrapped around his hips, just barely; his legs were shaved clean, his black wig on the dash so it wouldn't blow out the window.

I thumbed in the cassette he had in the player and it wasn't Breaking the Skin like I wanted to hear but the transcript of a high-school basketball game. Back Iron thumbed it back out, embarrassed.

In apology or thanks or both, I told him that I understood LP Deal now, why he didn't grow his hair out: because it weighed too much.

Back Iron laughed behind his hand.

'What do you think, then?' I asked.

'That he's the only one who cares what happened to coach,' he said.

'Because he found him.'

'Maybe.'

We drove. All I had heard on his tape so far was an announcer talking around a wad of quality frybread. He didn't know what quarter it was. I didn't ask.

Miles later I caught Back Iron watching me in the vanity mirror. 'Your eyes,' he said. My contacts. He was the only person in the world who would have noticed. In another setting I would have blushed, but Back Iron's tube top matched all the bracelets of his left wrist and some of them were mine.

'Gave them to Naitche,' I said, about the contacts, almost to myself, a joke, but it wasn't: Back Iron's oversized pump sagged off the pedal, the landscape snapping into focus behind him, catching up.

'What?' he asked.

It was his real voice; I had never heard it before.

In trade I mumbled my own name, but he said no, not that: before.

'I was joking,' I told him. 'They're on my sink, I think.'

Again, we drove. Outside what used to be Liberty Kansas Back Iron batted his fake eyelashes—they had to be fake—and told me that it wasn't his fault, Naitche. He had to wear them.

'The contacts,' I finished.

He nodded.

'But he's Indian,' I tried.

'Yeah, well,' Back Iron said, 'still, you know,' and then we were on Enil Anderson's road hours too soon, even for Back Iron.

'Wait here,' he said, stepping into a liquor store, showing too much thigh for three in the afternoon. His femurs had to go two feet at least. I covered my mouth and looked away, studied the shells in the gravel of the parking lot, all spiraling the same way. Except Naitche, immune, his white eyes cataloging, measuring, remembering.

Back Iron waved at me through the glass. He was at the end of the line, the center of attention. There was no better place to hide: two nights ago someone had spidered down through a museum vent on Old Pine Ridge with a tank of gas strapped to their back. It was for the faded red truck in the display case, one stray bullet hole crossing the bed, leaving a federal hole in each side. You could kneel down on the driverside and look through them both like a telescope, back to the past. Or stick your finger in them.

Back Iron was wearing a black leather glove on his right hand. He called it his driving glove, but it didn't go with anything, and he favored it, and I knew: the hole had been jagged.

He was buying champagne to celebrate.

I waved back to him then looked up, into the alcoholic haze above the liquor store, the buzzards riding the heat. My regulation issue .45 was miles away, the shiny mantelpiece of some den or living room in Broken Leg. The prairie-dog people probably didn't even sniff it anymore. Didn't even know me. This is what it's like to be undercover: you lean back in the seat of the car and shoot the buzzards one by one with your hand, then the prairie dogs, then you hold the barrel of the gun down to the tape in the tape deck, smile, pull that trigger.

Trans-Annie was the stage name of Enil Anderson's wife. It was like that in a clipping in the hall of their house. I don't know what her act was; the part of the article with specifics was shiny black with flies, as if the words had bulged, crowded into each other. LP would write like that if he could. I was already calling him LP by then, I guess.

I didn't say anything to Trans-Annie, either. Not that she would have listened. I did sit with her for three hours, though, until Back Iron appeared in the doorway, my full-length skirt whipping around his knees. I didn't know he'd brought that one; he was drunk, suddenly sober.

'Not your fault,' he said, about Trans-Annie, little Enil, but it was.

If I'd still had that feather, I would have left it there, with them, but all I could do was ride back to the Territories with Back Iron, pour champagne over the image of her at the end of Enil Anderson's driveway, on the other side of the front door, arranged on the couch to receive visitors, the cushions around her black with blood, her blood. And little Enil: he was the white child with his hands tied under the desk at Broken Arrow.

Her real name was Trudy, Trudy Anderson. The clipping in the hall said she was the opposite of Virginia Dare, whatever that meant. Enil Anderson knew: he had underlined it, his pen slashing the bottom off the *g* it was all balanced on.

He had never planned on coming home.

Back Iron left a bundle of sage burning in the dry aquarium, rescued the turtle from it, and then led me away, the fire alarm already keening. We drove faster than any Indians ever have. Dusk came; I could almost hear Mary Boy singing it up, his voice plaintive, earnest, but then it was night for miles and miles, until Yaqui Buoy. The attendant in his monochromatic coveralls was out in the road, in the dawn, all fingertips and toes, his ear to the asphalt, listening to us approach. I made Back Iron circle back through the weeds of No Man's Land but it wasn't him, LP Deal. But it was.

We stopped at the first motel and bought all the cedar and sage they had, and when we told the clerk we needed more he asked us to leave and I showed him my badge Back Iron said I really shouldn't be carrying and the clerk put everything on the counter into a parfleche cut from some great plastic cow and we hunched over it to the car, and because I couldn't anymore, Back Iron cried for me and we burned it all at once, the sage, the cedar, and it was sweet. The back glass exploded soundlessly.

We drove on, faster. Finally I screamed and put the black wig on over my blonde one, then took them both off, cut my real hair off in mourning, like I was supposed to. For Trans-Annie, Trudy Anderson. Her son.

The hair slipped out the window into birdnests and history and I fumbled the radio on, tuned in KORL, Oral Radio 93.7, 'keeping the tradition alive.' This morning it was a Bacteen story, some elder alone in the studio, afraid to touch the mic with his lips and die but talking anyway, talking. I closed my eyes and let his voice carry me.

| INDIAN BURN

This was a long time ago. Well, seven years,
maybe eight. It was the Moon of the Popping Bud.
So maybe January or February or April or Septem-
ber or October or December or November or March
or May or August, June or July. The sound a can
makes when it opens, right? Anyway, Bacteen
wasn't even drinking this day, which made him
notice how hungry he was. He was wearing his Big
Chief war shirt with all the bullet holes in it
and chewing some White Man. He could hardly talk
around it even, and finally took it out and
rolled it into the arms and legs and hump of a

buffalo, then buried it and made a fire over it.

'What are you doing?' Raven asked when he saw Bacteen.

'Cooking,' Bacteen said, and smiled.

Raven shook his head and flew away, saying he was glad to be a bird. At least he wouldn't get burned when Bacteen's fire got out of control again.

Bacteen stood over his fire.

Raven was right. Last time Bacteen had tried to cook he had burned down everything. But then Bacteen remembered what to do: he just had to offer some tobacco in the right directions. The tobacco was under the fire, though.

'I'll just take a little,' Bacteen said, and laid on his belly, dug under as far as his arm could reach, and cut off a little for the West.

'There,' he said, but then the world tilted to the West, so Bacteen reached under the fire again, cut off some tobacco for the East.

'Now,' he said, and squatted down over his fire. Just then Fox slid into his back, almost knocking him into the fire.

'What are you doing?' Bacteen asked him.

'Just riding,' Fox said, and took off running again, then jumped into a cannonball shape, kept sliding. Bacteen stood to see him better but almost fell forward. The world was tilted again, to the South.

He needed to offer more tobacco.

'But I won't have enough,' Bacteen thought, then reached under a third time anyway, used his scissors to cut off another piece of tobacco.

'I wonder what my buffalo looks like now,' he said, offering to the North. It knocked him back-wards, though—to the North. Bacteen was almost crying now.

'Well,' he said, laying on his belly again, reaching under the fire, 'one bite of buffalo will at least be better than no buffalo at all.'

And he offered the last piece to the South and
the world leveled out again, and he squatted over
his fire again singing the cooking song until the
buffalo should be done. But he couldn't reach it
anymore. He had cut too much off.

He called Raven to help, but Raven just
laughed.

He called Fox to help, but when Fox said yes
without asking for a bite, Bacteen knew Fox would
eat it, so he said thanks, but no.

Soon Coyote came nosing up.

'What you got there?' he asked.

'Nothing,' Bacteen said.

Coyote smiled. 'You need someone who can dig,'
he said, 'someone used to digging in holes.'

Bacteen stood. 'You're right,' he said, then
grabbed him—Coyote—and pushed his tail in,
smudged his eyes around, and made him into a
mole. 'Now you can get it,' he said, and the mole
growled, but did it, dived into the earth for the
buffalo, only when he came up his mouth was Coyote again. Bacteen hadn't pushed the nose in far
enough. Coyote was a badger now, not a mole. And
he had taken a fifth bite out of the tobacco, and
it wasn't a buffalo anymore.

'What is it?' Bacteen asked, and the badger
just stared at him.

'You can eat it,' Bacteen said—because Badgers
eat anything—but the badger shook his wide head
no and scampered away, looking back four times,
twice over each shoulder.

'I'll eat it then,' Bacteen said, and brushed
the dirt off. The tobacco still had four limbs,
but it was different. It was a man now. And
white. It reached up with a stick it had and
poked Bacteen in the eye, and Bacteen dropped
it.

They stared at each other, Bacteen rubbing his
eye.

'What are you?' Bacteen asked, but the thing just looked around.

'Thank you,' it said, and then dived back into the hole under the fire to cook some more.

Bacteen called Raven again and this time Raven landed and they looked in the hole together.

'What is it?' Bacteen asked, but Raven shrugged.

'Not a buffalo,' he said.

So they called Fox again. Fox smelled the air where the thing had been and shook his head.

'What'd you make it of, anyway?' he asked Bacteen, and Bacteen told him a plug of White Man, and Fox did that thing where he walks back and forth, his head and tail trading places, whipping back and forth.

'You shouldn't have done that,' he said.

Now they called Coyote.

Coyote padded up, stopping to smell this or that.

'Yes?' he said. He still had a poolstick in his hand from wherever he'd been.

'I cooked something wrong,' Bacteen said.

'No shit,' Coyote said. 'And it's loud, too.'

From the hole under the fire the thing was yelling. They couldn't understand it, though.

'What should we do with it?' Fox asked.

'Kill it,' Bacteen said, so they poured hot coals down there, but it wouldn't come up. They tried water, too, but the water just made steam. Raven said maybe they could bury it, but it still kept yelling under all the dirt.

'You need something that can dig,' Coyote said, and then turned back into a badger, dug the thing up, only this time he didn't eat any of it.

He sat it down in the middle of them all.

Fox tried to catch it in his mouth, but it was still too fast.

Bacteen tried to step on it, but it got away too, so he tried eight times with his scissors,

then eight more, but only got it at the edges of
its legs and arms, making fingers and toes.

'This is worse than the fire,' Fox said.

'What do we do?' Bacteen asked Coyote. 'We
can't kill it and we can't hide it and I can't
cook it anymore.'

'I can catch it,' Coyote said. 'I catch mice
all winter long.'

'Then do it,' Raven said.

'But I'm so sad,' Coyote said, dragging his tail.

'Why?' Fox asked. 'You're fast and can eat
anything.'

'And I already give you free haircuts...,'
Bacteen said, because he knew Coyote. But it was
too late.

'Yeah,' Coyote said, kicking a rock into the
fire. 'Everybody thinks I'm just a little wolf,
though.'

'Do you want to be bigger than Wolf?' Bacteen
asked, ready to stretch Coyote up.

Coyote shook his head no, though. 'Then I
wouldn't fit in my den,' he said, 'and I'd have
to eat more, work harder... No. Can you kill
Wolf, though, maybe? Then I wouldn't be 'little
wolf' anymore...'

Bacteen thought about it and thought about it—
because it would take him so long to kill all the
wolves, and he wasn't sure he could, anyway—and
then Raven whispered in Fox's ear and Fox whispered in Bacteen's ear and Bacteen whispered in
Coyote's ear that he would do it, just not right
away. But soon, if Coyote waited, all the wolves
would be gone, and the land would be full of
Coyotes, which is the way it already is now.

Coyote said yes to this, then pounced on the
thing, gave it to Bacteen, who tied him back into
the White Man package and told Raven to deliver
it as far away as he could, all the way across
the water.

But it came back.

Bacteen sat on the side of the road, still
hungry.

This was all his fault, he knew. He cut all
his hair off with his scissors, but it grew back,
so he cut it and cut and cut it, but he had more
grief than he did hair.

'I'll just leave,' he said, and stuck his
thumb out. Nobody was stopping for him, though.
Finally, he just laid his hand out in the road,
let a carload of tourists run over his thumb. It
swelled up nearly as long as his forearm and got
red as a stop sign. Now he had to hold it up,
because it throbbed if he didn't.

'Wonder what I'll pull over with this,' he
said, adjusting his vest, and when he looked up,
six American cars were stopped for him. The first
one was blue, the next red, and then white and
yellow and black and black again, with a red
stripe down the middle.

'More like a kite than a thumb,' the sixth
driver said to Bacteen, looking at his thumb, and
in trade for whatever food was in the glove compartment, Bacteen told them his secret, that
white people were just buffalo without any skin.
His proof was that as the white people appeared,
the buffalo disappeared, right? But it had only
looked like that. What had really happened was
they'd stepped out of their skins and built cities, but then got lonely for their skins, had to
start wearing them again, as robes.

The sixth driver held both hands on the wheel
and lowed like a buffalo bull.

They drove on in silence after that.

Bacteen didn't tell that one to the fifth
driver, either. Or the fourth or the third or
even the second, and then to the first he told
the truth: that the white people were buffalo
he'd cut all the good parts off of. His proof was

that they were white like bones, like a skeleton, right?

The first driver held both hands on the wheel and laughed, and his jaw came unhinged, fell down to his chest.

They drove on in silence after that.

Bacteen said to himself he was going to get out at the fourth intersection, but then stepped out at the first one while the car was still going, rolled in the ditch until nightfall.

'That's it,' he said, making the cut-off sign, 'no more,' but his thumb was still throbbing. As soon as he held it up, a bird landed on it and a carload of Americans stopped to take a picture, only Bacteen changed fingers at the last instant, even though it hurt. The bird flew away. He never knew what kind it was. It didn't matter.

Bacteen walked on, imagining his middle finger coming into focus in the watery pan of some dark-room in America. He practiced the move some more, without the bird—going thumb-finger, thumb-finger—but on the fourth time through, brake lights flared in front of him. It was an Indian pick-up truck, red on white.

Bacteen tried to wave it on but the truck followed him, even when he left the road. Finally he gave up after a few miles, waited for the truck to pull alongside.

Coyote was driving, his cowboy hat bent down nearly to the tip of his nose, his forearm on the top of the wheel, fingertips drumming the dash.

'So it's you,' Bacteen said, spitting on his thumb to cool it down.

'Where to, pilgrim?' Coyote asked, and Bacteen leaned back into the seat, looked all around at America.

'Back to before all this,' he said, and Coyote dropped the truck into gear.

SHIP OF fOOLS

The first thing you do is fall down. This isn't Coyote's pick-up anymore. This is the ocean. It's 1492.

'Not *this* far back,' you say.

You've got blue lines all over you, too, like tattoos but not. More like where to cut. On your back there are even two Cs, one for Christopher, one for Columbus. This is what it means when they used to say 'C to shining C': the prime cut, the backstrap. Standing all around are men in bad hair-cuts and clown pants. You don't know whether to wait for the elephants or get out your scissors. Instead you just laugh three times, once for yourself.

You're going west.

The things you cooked on accident are coming back across the water. And now you can stop them.

'What are you smiling at?' they ask you, and you just spit on your hands and rub the blue lines off your body.

'Nothing,' you say, then dive for the mast, climb up to the crow's nest to hatch a plan.

To the left and right behind are the Nina and the Pinta. There aren't any birds, either, because there's not any land. Yet.

Your plan is to foment something, a mutiny.

The white men are bigger than last time, though. You have to factor that in, that they won't fit in a tobacco pouch anymore. But they don't remember, either, which is good.

'Are you an Indian?' they call up.

'Yes,' you say, almost screaming with fear. 'How did you know?'

'Do you have any spices?' they ask.

'What are you going to put them on?' you ask back without looking over, but they don't answer. Which means you.

'I'm a barber,' you call back finally. 'Let me cut your hair and I can tie flies from it, and we can catch fish, and we can make keratin soup.'

After six days they agree, and come to you one at a time. Now you're in the bow of the ship, ahead of all of them. When you look behind you there are thousands of ships, and you tremble, cut half a sailor's ear off. He eats it.

You don't have long.

'You're hungry,' you tell him.

This is something you can use.

The hair you were cutting off him blows out to sea and you forget to pretend you were wanting it.

'Not going too well, is it?' you ask the next sailor. He shrugs.

'Where are you going, anyway?'

This is the third sailor, now.

'The edge of the world...,' you whisper, suggest, then, for the fourth sailor, teeter on the bow like you're about to fall off.

'It won't happen like that,' he says, eating the lice off the cut hair of the third sailor, but looks back once, too, unsure. You click the scissors at him.

The fifth sailor settles into the chair. You waft the old sail over him, tie it at the neck so he looks like he's in a canvas sack. He's bald but you snip anyway, lean down once or twice and ask him why he's here, starving? Just to prove Isabella wrong?

'Who?' he says.

'Done,' you say.

As the sixth approaches the chair you notice that now the sailors are gathering around the mast, talking in hushed tones.

Is this all it takes? Words?

You laugh again.

'What?' the sixth sailor asks.

'Just thinking of your...er, captain,' you say, and the two of you look at him together,

trying to tape the four corners of his map together so that it looks like a ball.

At the last moment you spin the chair around
so Columbus won't see the sixth sailor laugh. Not
yet. He walks away bald, chewing on the tip of
one of your fingers you forgot to get out of the
way.

It grows back like it always does.

Six days later it happens: the men rise up
with their good haircuts and tie Columbus to the
mast. His eyes are wild.

You're the captain now.

'So you want to go to India...,' you say, the
compass spinning in your palm.

The men nod, and for a moment you see a canine
snout in the crowd, but then it's gone and you're
steering: India; wherever.

Four days later they tie you to the mast with
Columbus.

'But we were *going* there,' you say, and Columbus smiles through his beard.

'They won't listen,' he says.

The next morning you see the first bird in
months. The men cheer, slice meat off your thighs
and sides, cook it with boards pulled up from the
deck. The other two ships are still following
you, and the rest, too. Their wake is so deep
that the sun's getting to bake the floor of the
ocean, and they're pushing up a tidal wave big
enough to crash across a continent.

Your thighs and sides grow back, and for the
next four days the men eat more and more of you,
until it doesn't hurt, until one of their knives
slips and cuts Columbus free.

He rolls across the poop and springs into
action, giving orders before anybody can remember
he's not the captain anymore. Soon they're in a
kickline singing a sailor song, their elbows
locked. Columbus sidles over for a Bacteen-filet,

and while he's cutting, says these men don't
deserve to live: he's going to sail them off the
edge of the damn world for mutinying against him.

You smile. 'Have some more,' you say, leaning
closer.

Maybe this was the plan all along: Isabella
just wanted to get rid of him, them, the trash of
Europe.

'What about the bird?' you ask him, the one
everyone saw four days ago.

'It was nothing,' Columbus says, chewing.
'Some birds spend their whole lives at sea, you
know that?'

You shake your head no, no.

'What are you really?' he asks you.

You look away. 'Food,' you say, ready to feed
them until the end of the world if you have to—
following the bird who never sees land—but later
that night the water changes, like at the edge of
a bathtub. Like it's hitting up against something.
Soon it's a sound, then a surf.

From the mast you can see the island, the
Indians.

'Run,' you tell them, and then down the beach
from them is a pair of headlights. They move out
across the water to you, the windshield wipers
spraying a salty mist up into the night.

Nobody sees you pull away from the mast, the
ropes. They're all in the bow, not dying, not
dead: here.

You shake your head no, no, not like this, not
like this, then run and dive into the water,
making a cannonball. Nobody notices.

Coyote slows down so you can climb in.

'Not just before America,' you tell him, and
he shrugs, flips his eyepatch up.

'When, then?' he asks.

'Longer ago,' you say.

BACK TO THE BLANKET

The plan you thought of tied to the mast had a
horse in it. It was beautiful: when the conquistadors glittered up onto the plains, the nations
there would sweep down on their painted Appaloo-
sas and the rest would be history, something to
talk about around the fire every winter. 'The
Time the Gold Men Came, Looking for Gold.' And
the children would smile like they didn't believe, then believe anyway.

And the Spanish horses would mingle with
theirs, and the buffalo runners would be the
stuff of legend.

But first you have to get one, bring it over.

And not by ship this time.

The first thing you do is fall down. You're
wearing muk-luks, the rest of you heavy with seal
hide, but the seals are months away. Months to
the east.

You smile, blow white air out your hood.

It's way before 1492. The lower steppes of the
Pastures of Heaven.

'Thank you,' you say to Coyote, wherever he
is. 'This is more like it.'

You fold the hood back, hold your ear to the
ground, and can feel the horses running. The next
day you trace your fingers over their tracks. The
third day you find an old campfire, the stones
done all wrong, and then on the fourth day
there's a scooped-out log with a dead woman inside. The fifth day you stay away from every
tree, and then on the sixth day you find them,
the live ones, signaling to each other across the
foothills with mirrors.

They're white too, almost. 'They've already
wrapped around the world,' you think. 'Like a
snake.'

Because they don't know about Indians over
here, it's easy to creep into camp, lead all

their horses away. But then when you're almost
gone you angle your hood wrong and the sound of a
baby crying gets trapped in there.

You take all of the horses back but one, so
the baby won't starve, but the sound is still in
your hood, so you let the last one go, too.

It was supposed to be easier than this.
They're just white people. But still.

That next night the parents of the baby pass
it from lodge to lodge, and each time it changes
hands, it grows, until it's ten almost. And then
it comes out to you at the fringe of the camp.

'You wanted a horse,' she says.

You nod.

She smiles, touches your scissors. 'You didn't
have to come all the way over here, silly,' she
says, then chases a bird into flight. When she's
gone you look at your scissors, and walk, and use
them to cut bushes out of the way. *The leaves of
some of them are like horses' ears*, the girl
calls out, and she's right. They are. So you cut
the rest into a horse head, then a horse body,
then cup your hand around the flared nostrils,
breathe into them.

The horse snorts, whinnies, stomps.

You talk it across Siberia, to the bridge of
land and ice, and then across it. Out in the fog
the People ghost by in their whalebone boats,
their paddles inches from the water.

'I'm bringing you the horse,' you call out to
one of them.

'What does it taste like?' he whispers back.

Your voice has already calved a block of ice
into the water. It floes by. The whalebone boat
rocks back and forth.

'It's not for eating,' you tell him, and pull
the horse away from his harpoon, already testing
the flesh. You follow the shore south, always
south; determined.

The second person you see is squatted over a
stream, his spear cocked, waiting for a fish.

His eyes are the only part of him that moves.

'Big dog you got there,' he says.

'It's not a dog,' you say. 'It's a horse.'

The man laughs without moving his lips. 'What
are you supposed to do with it?' he asks.

'Ride it,' you say, stepping on.

'Where?' the man asks.

All around is trees, trees. Nowhere to run.
You do anyway, kick the horse south, out of the
trees, into the desert where the third man is.
He's braiding some grass outside his lodge.

'It's not a dog,' you tell him before he can
ask.

'Why is it looking at me like that?' the man
asks.

'Like what?'

You get down, but the horse is just looking.

'How much water does it drink?' the man asks.

You shrug, let the horse nose into a clay jug
in the shade. It drinks it all. The man stands,
looks at the horse, the sun.

'That was all my water for the rest of the
year,' he says.

You look down, then to the west, where the
sky's blue with rain. 'I'm sorry,' you mumble,
and ride to the storm. The grass there rubs the
horse's belly and the bottom of your feet.

The fourth man is at the edge of another camp.
He stumbles outside when he hears the horse's
hooves, and his wife follows, carrying their
baby.

'Why is he so skinny?' you ask—the baby.

'Because we don't have any food,' the man
says.

You pat the horse. 'With this you can catch
all the buffalo you want.'

The man smiles at the horse.

'What does it taste like?' he asks, and you look to his wife, his baby, his baby, his baby, and tell him you don't know, and then hand him the reins.

'We don't have anything to give you,' he says, tying the horse to a rock. 'Wait till the morning, though.'

That night you sit outside their lodge and watch the shadows of them on the thin skin of the lodge. The air around them is their fire; they're eating the horse. You smile, almost, then watch as they pass the baby from lodgepole to lodgepole. It grows up into a little boy already, but then hunches over on the ground, its nose getting longer.

Coyote.

In the morning he's leaning against his truck, cupping a cigarette from the wind.

'So?' he says.

'I couldn't let them starve,' you say.

'What about the rest of them, then?' he asks.

Already you can see the conquistadors' helmets glittering to the south, their armor too hard for flint.

Coyote shrugs, climbs into the cab, unlocks the door for you. While the truck's warming you unroll your BDU jacket from behind the seat, put it on like you're going to hide in America some more. Again. When you lean back, though, your head hits a gun in the gunrack.

You laugh four times, all for yourself.

'What?' Coyote asks, shifting gears, the grass rushing along the floorboard, and you tell him to wait, you'll be right back, then roll out the passenger side door, into 1845.

NO SOUVENIRS

This time would be different. What they needed was this, the gun: the repeating rifle. Fuck Remington; this was a Savage.

The first thing you do is fall down. The next thing is stay there, and stay there, holding your hip where it took the butt of the rifle. Like you can cover the pain. The barrel is full of dirt. The truck is a brown plume, already blowing away.

This is still the grassland, at least. Home.

There are eight shells in the gun.

Two of them you use on one rabbit, and eat alone that night. Another you fumble into a prairie-dog hole. The fourth you keep in the chamber. The rest go in a pouch around your neck.

The rabbit is greasy and perfect. In the morning you stuff the skin full of grass, stand it up in the coals of the fire. It jumps out. You smile.

Home.

From a ridge you can see teepee rings to the north, so you go the other way, to meet whichever band it is that makes this circuit every year.

Three days out, there they are.

You carry the rifle first by your leg, then on your back, then behind your neck like a stick—any way but like a soldier. They don't take it from you, just feed you instead, wait for you to talk.

It takes a while, though; you want to stay here, silent, just moving along. But then on the second night one of the children pulls the trigger of the rifle and the fourth shell makes a hole in the lodge. The darkness seeps in, the smoke rising to meet it.

'So,' you say, fingering your pouch, the one on your neck.

They're all looking at you, even The Half—the impossibly tall one who wears his face and chest painted like they say his father's was when they found him: with black paint across the eyes like sunglasses, a stripe down the chest for a tie. Black leggings, black war shirt. His hair parted not in the middle but the side.

You hold the rifle out in your fist. 'You want
to keep this land?' you ask.

They shrug as one: of course.

'This, then,' you say, the rifle. 'This is
what you need.'

'How much?' one asks.

You tell him it's a gift.

'It's a gun,' another says, sighting down it
at an imaginary buffalo.

You nod, tell him it's better, though. Show
him the lever action.

Now they're nodding too.

'And we just need one?' a third asks.

The Half is looking at you. You look at the
gun for an answer, and there it is: 'You just
have to build more like this,' you say.

The Half smiles, looks away, and you break the
rifle down into receiver, barrel, trigger shroud;
firing pin, bolt, lever; stock, tube. The pieces
are everywhere. It takes you six days to get them
back together, and then it's not even you, but
The Half. He does it without looking.

'How do you know?' you ask. 'This isn't even
invented yet...'

He shrugs, adjusts the painted-on sunglasses.
'My father, I guess,' he says.

He's married to an Indian woman, the tallest
of the band. Their children will be tall too, and
their children's children, and on and on until
now.

'Who was he?' you ask, though, 'your father.'

'Q'uan-the-kho,' he says, like it's nothing,
then spits the rest: 'A white man.'

With the rifle together he sights out into the
distance, on an imaginary white man. But they're
not imaginary anymore, by then.

'Does it work now?' one of the old men asks,
and you finger the last four shells in, and they
follow you out into the grasslands. Two of the

young men are buffalo callers. They spread their robes, flap them, sing, and in two days a herd darkens the land.

'Thank you,' you say.

'Which one?' you ask the old man, and he selects a cow at the edge of the herd. You sight in on it, push a round into its side, then, before it can even fall, lever two more out there. And a strange thing happens: the whole herd shudders, looks at you as one, their eyes rimmed red.

'I'm sorry,' you say, but the old man has the rifle now, is lining up on another tender cow.

'No,' you say, but he does, knocks her down.

That was the last shell, the formula for gunpowder. The shot goes around the world.

'Fuck Remington,' you say, quietly, ducking from the slug, still circling, and The Half looks down at you from his great, shaggy height.

'It wouldn't have mattered,' he says. 'Did you want us to stand on an assembly line, making them?'

He doesn't understand, though: this is all your fault. You have to fix it.

The next day in a sweat, the rifle bundled up in otter pelt with buffalo stones and feathers and sage, a chert point already tied over the sights, you try to breathe it all in, get all the way clean, but when the stones are cold you're alone.

The rabbit you built noses into the short lodge, its nose twitching, and it comes to you: you should build a *man* like that, fill him full of vaccine and foreknowledge, hide him in the back of Coyote's truck then push him out...

This time you don't eat the rabbit, just stand knee-deep in the grass of the past and wait for the headlights, but when they come, pushing through four days of buffalo, you shake your head no, no.

'Not yet,' you say, and turn hard, run east in great loping strides, to Philadelphia, twenty years later.

It's not too late.

I SAW A BUFFALO ROAM

And you're not going to have to build a straw man. You make enough people on accident already, right?

It's not cold yet in Philadelphia, either, which is good: your plan isn't to save the Indians anymore, but the buffalo.

The American name you give at the hat shop is Sweeney Todd, like always. The hat is a bowler. It looks good with your jacket. You tip the hatmaker a used lambskin you had in your pocket, but tell him it's a baby muskrat.

He stands holding it to his face in front of the mirror and you walk out into the bustle of the city.

The first thing you do is fall down.

This is the year that the Anti-trickster Buffalo Bill is supposed to kill nearly four thousand head. You don't tell him he's shooting his own kind, that it's suicide, but you do, too, he just doesn't hear over the sound of his gun.

It doesn't matter. If you can make nobody want to wear them, then people will just shoot them for railroad meat, and maybe one night soon Buffalo Bill will rest the octagonal barrel of his long rifle against the roof of his mouth, pull the trigger with the toe of his show boot, paint the world Red again.

With your head against the brick street you can hear all this happening, see it almost. And then someone steps on your hand, and someone else, so you follow them, hold them between your knees like sheep, give them a haircut they won't ever forget, or remember, or tell anybody about.

The papers talk about their smiling necks but it's not you. You're here just because Philadelphia is the fashion capital of the New World, the Old Northwest. You walk through the streets in clothes so crisp they crackle, and you're whistling, just so you won't have to smell the filth and decay. It'll be worse if they shoot all the buffalo again, though.

You keep telling yourself this.

The barber in the city of brotherly love. That's what they're calling you. At night in your bed you snip your scissors in the lamplight, long for the Declaration, the Constitution, the Indian Removal Act. Or just the men themselves.

But you're not here for that.

The buffalo.

Your clothes are waiting outside your room in the morning and you step into them, approach the bar where the fashionable huddle in fear that if they can't see each other, one of them might get ahead, be the first to wear the new thing.

Call it Trendsetters, the bar, but it isn't.

You can still hear that baby crying. And the buffalo are still looking at you and their eyes are the eyes of the Arawak of San Salvador, before it was San Salvador.

You are the exact opposite of civilization.

'Hide your daughters,' you mumble liplessly, then push the doors of the bar open, stride in.

You're just what they've been waiting for. They all turn into fawns that afternoon, and as the day turns into a week they mature into timid does, then they go in heat and will believe anything you say.

Sweeney Todd educates them on the vulgarity of wearing the skin of animals—the lice, the disease.

'Are you Indian or are you white?' you ask them.

They're white. But still, they look down their
arms, step out of their shoes, drop them into the
fire. The polished leather hisses.

'That's more like it,' you say, and then, for
emphasis, pull a barbarian off the street. He's
fresh from the west, a real mountain man.

'What's that he's wearing?' one of the women
asks.

'Buffalo,' you say, curling your lip.

'Lower,' another says. On his belt.

Scalps. Black hair with flecks of face paint
balled in the forked ends.

'Exactly,' you say, swallowing. 'Would you
wear the skin of another person?'

'Person?' they say.

You smile.

'Indian,' you correct.

They shake their heads no, but it's because
the Indians live off the buffalo, have the same
lice, the same disease.

You tell yourself it doesn't matter, but it
does.

That night the mountain man's too far in his
glass to see you coming, either. One more for the
papers.

'You're right,' the people at the bar murmur,
about the animal skins, that they're not barbar-
ians. It's a lie you can live with.

You rent a chair in the warehouse district
just to pass the time, watch it all come down.
And it does: with winter comes wool coats for the
wind, not buffalo robes. When Kansas sends its
first load of stiff hides to the train station,
nobody's there to pick them up, and they attract
flies, spread disease. It's perfect. You stand at
the edge of the rotting mass and say thank you,
for their sacrifice.

By the end of the day the flies have blotted
out the sun, and then they drift into Philadelphia

proper, and the next day in the paper, between
flies mashed in the huge rollers, is an article
about uncleanliness, distance from their bearded
God. Punishment. Just reading the paper gets
people violently ill. Four die, with assistance,
and the rest stumble through the streets, retch-
ing from the flies they've inhaled. The gutters
run white with maggots, and in the wake of all
this a soap salesman peddles into town, cleans
up. The money comes to him hand over fist.

He smiles.

Do you recognize him? The moustache? Blue
eyes?

You offer him a free haircut to look closer
but he twists his limp handlebar and declines,
politely, so politely.

This was the year the southern herd was supposed to disappear, you tell yourself. And it
hasn't. And that's good.

But then.

The soap peddler buys a warehouse to better
serve the unclean, the compulsive handwashers who
remember the flies, and when his New York suppli-
ers miss a delivery, he looks elsewhere. To the
Plains.

'No,' you say, trying to get a customer's
cowlick to lie down with saliva, but the soap
peddler's already seen a new supplier.

What he needs as a base for his soap is something chalky and fine, available in limitless
amounts.

What he gets are buffalo bones.

In the paper he explains how it's Native
ingenuity—using the whole beast, wasting not—but
he's no Indian.

'It won't last,' you say to the next customer,
and when he doesn't agree you snip the top of his
ear accidentally on purpose, but it's already
gone: he's the sailor from the Nina, the Pinta,

the Santa Maria, whichever one you were on. The
one who ate his own ear. And then you.

There are ways to die where you still walk,
talk, shave people, your straight razor so close
to their uneven throats.

In a matter of weeks the plains are black with
boneless hides and wasted meat. Now the flies are
there, the buffalo on silver trays in the bathrooms. You collect them for weeks, sing to them
at night, and finally, as has to happen, you
start washing your hands until they crack open
and bleed, and then you try to wash the blood
off, and then a man sits down in your chair, his
hair reddish-grey and shaggy and down to his
belt. Like he's made of it.

'Just a little off the top,' he says.

And you do it, and somewhere in there he asks
if you've heard about the Conservation projects,
the reintroductions. That the wolves are coming
back.

It's so silent you can hear his sharp teeth
touching each other in a wide, blacklipped grin,
a coyote smile.

You cut the rest of the hair, and it's Him.

He removes the dropcloth, folds it over the
back of the chair.

Past the plate glass is modern Wahpeton, the
truck nosed up to the curb, windows down.

'Where to now?' he says, leaning over the
wheel again, waiting for the lighter to pop back
into his waiting hand.

'Just drive,' you tell him.

On the way back into the Territories he breaks
his cigarette open, trails it out the window like
you're supposed to. His hair is perfect. It's the
only thing.

keep off the grass

no.

Birds of a Feather

PINK EYE was all the rage. It was a heathen condition, the second since Conservation. The first had been teeth, because Indians have a different kind of root, don't come from the same place as Americans. I remember my uncles all wearing one of their incisors on a string around their necks. It was an ID badge; they talked like the sixth grade. The women, though—my aunts—they bought molars and canines in bulk from winos and wore them dangling from their ears, and still flash their white smiles to the toothless men huddled in front of the liquor stores, the blood from their dry sockets blooming in their brown bags like grenadine. We used to call them in as Bleeding Gums and No Teeth and Whistler, remember? And it was funny then. Before Trans-Annie. All of her teeth had been in a china bowl on the coffee table, though, Blue Plume. Because you can't tell without pulling them.

She wasn't Indian. Neither was her son. And my eyes were so white after seeing her; I was bleached on the inside. But there are ways. There are always ways.

On the edge of the bed were Back Iron's diva sunglasses. The ones he wore on bad make-up days. Like today was going to be, after driving all night. I didn't chase him down, though, even though I could hear that he'd found the basketball rolled up against the trashcan, was trying to dribble it out the window as he backed up. It would take him all day to get to his trailer. And he hadn't really left them, anyway. I had just wanted them; stole them.

This is when I quit being a cop, I guess, out at the edge of Two Burn Flat, on the way back from America. There had been a borrowed car upside down in the ditch, still trailing streamers and beer cans, *just married* smeared across the back glass. It was the only thing not broken. I already knew I wasn't going to call it in, too. It was the way Back Iron was slowing, lowering his sunglasses to see if it was anyone he knew. A shimmery white veil clung to the torn exhaust and he whimpered once with desire, and I nodded, and that was when he rested his sunglasses on the dash and wiggled out of his skirt, into the grassland.

He approached the car from upwind, feinting, bobbing, flirting, and just as he was reaching his long arm across the smoking chassis for the impossible veil, a doe looked up at him over the passenger side of the car, stared at him with her eyes and with her ears, and he smiled back with his whole face, looking from her to the white fabric, billowing out longer than any manufacturer could have guaranteed. His lips moved after a while but I don't know in what language, just that he wasn't reaching for the veil anymore.

'Why didn't you get it?' I asked him when he was back.

'It wasn't mine,' he shrugged, shouldering into the flimsy straps of his halter top. The sun was so bright on the hood, too, but he didn't say anything, and I didn't say anything. Not out loud. We just squinted ourselves closer to the tectonic parking lot of Broken Arrow, 219b, and he deposited me onto the asphalt plate by my room, and we were already drifting apart. The next place I would see him would be on the postcard everybody probably knows about by now, the holographic one of him in a black wig and Denim Horse's manclothes, standing in the open door of the fugitive red truck, arms crossed, the heel of one of his boots hooked up onto the running board. In the picture the truck is parked in the silvery tall grass and he's waiting for you to walk closer, get in with him—*leave*, like a father with visiting privileges for the weekend—but when you tilt it, it's not him in the hologram anymore, but an Old One on his chrome horse, the butt of his spear on the ground, a fist made around the middle of it. They're the same person, though.

I figured this all out too late, too. In the laundry room with Cat Stand. It was the first place I'd worn the sunglasses. Instead of harsh whites, the place was tinted grey like the afterlife, the sandhills. Like looking through the veil Back Iron didn't have. Enil Anderson and the other thirty-nine were crowding close to me; the washers all clicked into dirge cycle. I stuffed the reds and the whites in, unable to distinguish, and slammed the door down over them, held it closed with my forearms, my face in my hands. I hadn't slept in I don't know how long.

Cat Stand was dipping her flannel into the soapy water one piece at a time. And watching me like she wanted to say something.

This is the interview, yes. But not yet.

First, the tape I listened to at the liquor store the day before. It had been Owen82's last game. Back when he wasn't Owen82 yet. Which isn't where it started—*this*: Nickel Eye, Fool's Hip, LP Deal—but it's one place, anyway.

The tape.

I pushed it in and it came back out. Twice we did it, and finally I slapped it on the dash and made the face you're supposed to make. It was padded, though—the tape—insulated with names, four layers of adhesive labels stacked like stairsteps. The outermost was *The Bad River Band: Hoopin' it Up*, then right under that *Naming Ceremony: 38.R-934b*, then *Algonquin Phonics: Getting Primitive*, and then the original, a handwritten *Trading Buckets*, with the date.

Hoopin' it Up was just a smuggler's pun—Back Iron laughing inside that it really *was* about basketball, then easing back into the Territories, one hand over the wheel, eyelashes curling up into the headliner. And the *Phonics*-one, no tollbooth guard would ever confiscate that unless you were going *in*to the Territories. Under it was the real one, though: *Trading Buckets*, which had at one time— for a few years, probably—become *38.R-934b*.

Which is what made me double-dribble the tape into the floorboard.

The files we used to trade the Hotline for had the same hierarchy of numbers and letters, right? Meaning the anthropologists had wanted this tape—how Owen82 got his name. And somebody had rubbed that *Phonics*-label on and carried it across to them. Some tomato. And then Back Iron had dropped down into their data warehouse on the narrow beam of a penlight, done his thing.

How did he *know*, though?

And who was he protecting?

I listened to the tape and watched him move ahead in line one Indian at a time, in fits and starts. He knew I was listening too, but I couldn't stop, was into it already. It was his and Denim Horse's last chance. The hardwood floor, the crowd, winter just outside the gym, fry bread warm in the air, with a song.

The old-time Indians never had this.

I turned it up just as Eddie Dial drifted out onto the court, his champion Diné in a ragged V behind him, passing a ball back and forth like weaving a rug. He was their point guard; it was his second senior year, even, according to whichever announcer wasn't eating or in the bathroom. His main post was a lanky tall white kid, number 32, only he'd had his mother or sister sew in an *n* and a *d* after it, which made him a *32ⁿᵈ*, which meant that back in the 1840s or sometime one of his grandparents had been Indian, the other just tall.

And the Warriors, the twin towers, Denim Horse and Back Iron, still mirror images back then, interchangeable in Owen82's offense. In the pre-game warm-up Denim Horse jogged in for a lay-up with Back Iron on the rebound, and for a moment, as they passed under the basket, they were one person and everyone saw it and one woman almost cried (me).

The first quarter was just what the tape said: trading buckets. Up one end, down the other, Owen82 giving the crowd all the sideline theatrics they could ask for. Twice Back Iron had the chance to slam on a loping breakaway, and twice he tucked his feet up under him, finger-rolled. All the announcers could talk about was the 32ⁿᵈ, though, lighting it up from long range, inside, kissing it off the glass Indian style. Once he even threw one up from the bench, and it would have slashed through the net and brought the house down if Denim Horse hadn't goal-tended on a reluctant nod from Owen82.

He was wearing his hair down even then, too, Denim Horse, carrying his head the same way—like his hair was a hood he was looking out of—Back Iron consciously imitating him, setting the Diné up for their fourth quarter soap opera move, where they would switch twins, put the one who could handle the ball at the top of the key instead of down low, let him crossover on the 32ⁿᵈ and float it into a sea of flashbulbs, drawing all the contact he could.

It would have worked, too, except for Eddie Dial. But that was later, in the fourth quarter. With fingernails. This was the closing seconds of the second, though, the drums under the stands pounding, making you *want* to dribble, focusing everything on that one hail mary from the Diné, the first announcer rising from his chair, scraping past the microphone, mumbling *sorry* to the second announcer on his way up.

Sorry.

I don't know if that ball ever made it.

Sorry.

It was like in one of the old black and white ethnology documentaries, where they're in some elder's house, and he's playing wise and savage all at once for them, but then, as he's walking out the door, he stops to straighten the rug with his cane. And the camera lingers, unsure.

I rewound, rolled the volume to the right, relistened: again, *sorry.* But now there was something just before that. Like the clattering of a wire, or glass; sunglasses. The first announcer had knocked the second's sunglasses off. And it was winter, and indoors, and then I saw it, heard it: *hail mary.* Not a thing you could get away with saying those first years, especially over a loudspeaker. That's what the first announcer had called it, though, giving himself away. And I should have recognized him all along, I was just so used to him talking about cheeseburgers and open lanes over the system at Fool's Hip.

Mary Boy, the red Catholic. The crowd trilling all around him.

Maybe this wasn't about Owen82. And maybe they had all been there—Courtney Peltdowne a Charity Striper at halftime, with their peekaboo kickline; LP Deal the tollbooth guard who scuttled out after them, lowering his head to the ground to listen for the approaching teams, then nodding to the crowd yes. They were coming. Cat Stand working concessions, Naitche unborn. Nickel Eye standing by the door, or shuffling through the round dance. Or maybe the other announcer.

I fast-forwarded over the rest of the game: Eddie Dial rising to mark Denim Horse's face in the fourth quarter, Back Iron trying to scratch his own the same way; the crowd chanting *Owen82, Owen82*; the Warriors cutting off another half inch of hair; all the elders sighing out into the snow, not looking at each other.

'I don't know why they were there, even,' a voice said.

It was Owen82.

I closed my eyes, didn't want to see him, didn't want him to be there. Didn't want his hand to settle over mine on the glove compartment, tell me it was alright.

'Please…,' I started to say, shaking my head no, trying to swallow, breathe, do *some*thing with my throat, but then he went on—gruff, defeated. Coming out of the speakers, off the tape. I didn't touch it. This was years later. He was on the phone it sounded like. '…thing about wanting to see if one was better than a half, if the FBI was going to win this time, or the Indians. Bullshit if you ask me. They were *all* Indians, I mean, even that white kid.'

'…'

'No. They're not related. They were Lakota, he was, I don't know, Navajo a long time back.'

'…'

'Diné, then. Whatever. He could shoot, I mean. Not like Michael, but still.'

'…'

'No, *Michael*. And Thomas.'

'…'

'Far as I know Michael's still got leukemia and all that. Thomas, though, him. That one never left the gym, you know. Some kids just get addicted like that, can't get enough. That one he just traded in his shoes for some regalia—' and then the tape stopped. I nearly fell into the dash. Back Iron was standing at the end of the hood, holding a bag on his hip, the neon lights of the liquor store behind him hazing his hard edges, like radiation. Like leukemia.

I looked away, to Denim Horse back then, while Back Iron—*Michael*—had been in the hospital. Owen82 was right: he never left the gym, won every fancy-dance trophy there was, until they started to model them after him. And Back Iron, he had to shave his head in physical mourning for his own bones, see his face in the newspapers after every pow-wow, in the shroud of Denim Horse's hair, then rub his hand over his own smooth scalp, look down the hall.

And I couldn't tell Cat Stand any of this.

That I stole Back Iron's sunglasses mostly because I couldn't steal the tape.

That I knew Naitche was watching us through the plate glass of the laundry room, his hands on the sill like it was a console, like this was all a big video game; like we had that many lives.

That Back Iron was still standing in the doorway, looking down the hall.

That it was the same hospital she'd been at.

He was fresh from treatment, walking down the hall to the duffle bag or closet or wherever he found the fancy-dance regalia. Or maybe he was holding it for Denim Horse while Denim Horse was in town, at the bar, in a motel room, with a nurse. Back Iron's room was a locker.

He put the leggings on, the bustle, the roach, tied them all down.

You couldn't tell his skin was crawling with heat, his cells writhing, his pupils blown wide with anticonvulsants.

He was Denim Horse; Denim Horse was him. It was what coach had always said: that you could trade them. You could, when you had to, when your body hurt too much to stay in it.

He looked down his long arms, turned his forearms up then down. Moved the toe of a moccasin. Breathed out through his nose.

Denim Horse.

The one who didn't have leukemia.

He stepped out of his room, pushed himself from wall to wall down the hall, an apparition. People leaned on their walkers and watched him pass, and he flashed his teeth, stumbled on like he knew where he was going. Where he had to go. He was Denim Horse; he found her room without any help. Second floor, the sheets changed daily for however many years already. She'd grown since Arizona, too. Since the rodeo, the bad luck bleach he'd found in some livestock show kit.

It was going to be funny.

Standing in the doorway, he laughed, stumbled into the room, shook his head no: he wasn't that boy anymore. He was Denim Horse. She was Cat Stand. They belonged together.

This is how things happen. Dyed feathers on sterile sheets, leaving a painted outline of him on top of her, like she had been standing in the way of a powerful radiation, and it had left a white shadow behind her.

God.

One of the things I didn't tell him after he left that veil for the doe was that the doe had had one blue eye, one brown, like Naitche. That I understood.

But I didn't, either.

And the sterile sheets of the hospital were tumbling linen now, in the dryers all around us, me and her. Cat Stand.

She was draping her flannel into the soapy water one piece at a time. And watching me like she wanted to say something. And I was terrified of what her voice might sound like after all these years.

On the other side of the plate glass Naitche scraped away. We both watched him.

'Game over,' I said, almost to myself, but she heard, almost smiled. Started in the middle.

Her voice was perfect.

calling the pope
                     'like that and the whole way there
rusting in the ditches and up on blocks where theyd been
stripped and turned over in the fields were the cars and
the trucks and the recreation vehicles still sitting
where theyd rolled some end over end some the traditional way some in ways only indians could have ever
thought of like having a coathanger for an antenna only
the part that used to hook over the rod or pole or
whatever it is in the closets is bent off to the side for
better reception which isnt just an accident waiting to
happen but a tight little visual of the day of the parade
the whole thing in miniature and it all comes down to a
carload of people officially whooping it up at ninety

miles per hour the driver lying about this time he got so
close to a telephone pole that it took the passengerside
mirror off or at least folded it in or shattered the
glass out the screaming reflection of the passenger but
the thing is that was how *close* he got only this guys
been drinking ever since they heard the announcement on
the grocery store radio about conservation and just left
their baskets of dry goods cocked in the aisles their
middle fingers cocked at the security cameras their car
cocked in the parking lot waiting for the driver to
misremember conser*va*tion as conver*sa*tion miles down the
road and start lying about this telephone pole thing
until one of the backseat crowd calls him on it which is
bad news because what they say is that indians all they
had left then after their land had all been taken was
their pride which is the thing that makes the driver ease
over into the ditch at ninety miles per hour the territories or what will be the territories almost in sight
but he just wants to *ding* the mirror a bit on a fence
post or a reflector just to show the asshole in the
backseat who just found them in the parking lot anyway
but its taking miles to prove his point now to prove that
he *can* that he *did* that he wasnt lying and the fence
posts wont stay still for him and might be too short
anyway so he sets his sights on the telephone pole again
and when hes almost there just when that one in the
backseat is thinking *shit shit shit hes gonna do it he*
wasnt lying that hooked finger part of the coathanger
antenna catches the guidewire of the telephone pole like
its the rod in gods closet in heaven and even though in
the past this car has had doors fall off just from
shutting them and headliners drape down over everyone
just when the sirens flashed and wheels fall in the night
when no one was looking leaving the car high centered on
its own muffler a seesaw for kids still the broken base
of this antenna is planted deep like its coiled around
the frame the very being of this car and the part of the
coat hanger tied around the chrome stump and squeezed
there with vice grips doesnt snap off either like it
really really should but lifts the front of the car off
the ground at the same incline as the wire only it
completes what the wire doesnt by flying off into the sky
for a few twisting moments crushing everyone inside when
it lands even the guy going *shit shit shit* and back then
fourteen years ago it must have flared up into a bonfire

too because the grass is still greener around it maybe
from the nitrogen that follows a burn maybe from the
human flesh turned again into dirt maybe from other
people stopping to close their eyes and pee behind it but
there are mounds of these rusting cars on the way into
the territories like the beaches of florida all the
contraptions the cubans use to get across the indians
were just like that during the parade sometimes even
cannibalizing the wrecked cars for alternators and link-
ages and tape decks before the national guard could
clean the dead people out and deliver them to their
families with no ceremony but they the indians never
took anything before tying something to the car in trade
maybe dusting an arm or a hand or whatever was crushed
out the window with cornmeal or leaving a wedge of liver
or the best bite of a ritual hamburger there but they
probably didnt have time to sing because they were going
there too just *on* the road and *right* side up and *with*
their organs on the inside of their bodies but still they
sang it in their head trying to get those people home or
back and for a while if the news didnt lie (i wasnt
there) for a while the radio stations even sang some of
the old songs live not recorded and the people in their
cars held their wheels with both hands and the hooked
parts of their coathanger antennas picked the voices out
of the air and then they were bursting through andrews
point and yaqui buoy before it was yaqui buoy and bends
twice and dont look back and bright eyes and then having
to huddle in the makeshift booths filling out the *appli-
cations* to be indian and proving it with old turtle
rattles and scars and dances they knew and stories they
didnt and the television crews were there from america
like buzzards youd want to say only we werent dead so
they left but thirteen years later when we crossed there
was still the smell only now it was from the hotels
strung out like beads along no mans land and not even one
hotel had windows on the east side of the building
anymore but still there was glass from sill to sill which
was anthropologists and ethnologists and enthusiasts
stacked belly to back watching through binoculars their
saliva coating the bricks for stories and stories and
naitche counted them all in a disinterested glance and
added them and subtracted them down to nothing and didnt
tell me how many were watching just looked away to the
anasazi at the tollbooth (yaqui buoy) down on fingertips

and toes listening to us or pretending to and naitche leaned forward smiling and the car didnt hit the anasazi like it could have and really he wasnt even the anasazi then was just some guy in a brown jumpsuit that was supposed to look like buckskin probably only the brass zipper down the middle was a giveaway and this is what im telling you that while i was filling in the application he clowned around outside for naitche and even got him to smile which caught in my throat for some reason and made me stand from the table where i *wasnt* writing where id been (television comatose unconscious poisoned raped pregnant america) not for anybody or changing my name either and thats when deep in the territories a glint rose off a windshield or a chrome bumper and the anasazi saw it too and made a show of seeing it for naitche and later when naitche would ask me about him about the anasazi hed said he was i would say that there were no anasazi anymore which probably wasnt good because he needs lies to believe in maybe we all do like that he could have risen from the asphalt after but he did too to fools hip ahead of us somehow after he scanned my application and told me his joke about immaculate reconception and calling the pope but by then that chrome bumper from the territories was a sound only it hadnt been a bumper at all but a *whistle* polished and repolished by the man driving with his hands clenched around the wheel his head straight ahead and the thing was he stopped which you dont have to do just to leave but he did because the anasazi was down on his fingertips and toes again horsing around for naitche but then having to follow through some to make it look official approach the window and all that and because the door of the booth was still open the drivers voice came across that he was learning al*gon*quin could he please just pass which slowed the anasazi for a moment because it didnt make sense and there was something wrong with his voice anyway the drivers and then the anasazi just kept standing there and standing there looking into the car until something *had* to happen like first us pulling away slow and unauthorized and then him the anasazi stepping back from the car and waving it on waving it away like he didnt care whatever just go go go then turning for us still down the road already and holding his hand up like we can still fix this its not too late it was nothing and all for naitche just for how it would look just to make him smile

he put his ear to the ground again only he was looking
the wrong way and never saw

quetzalcoatl
the plumy god the feathered serpent who
wasnt the pope but might have been good enough that day
with his quills and his green light and his eyes and i
even said his name once (thomas cortes) when i was famous
on all the television sets across america and in return
he lifted me up with him into the sky and flew across the
rodeo grounds on bare feet across all of arizona into a
line at a supermarket that took all day because of the
abandoned baskets in the aisles and the rotting food in
the baskets and our car was cocked out in the parking lot
and naitche had the inventory of the whole store of the
whole town of the whole country in his head by now
already when the cashier poured the change into my hand
only one of the coins was false was a token was *him* at
fools hip and naitche rolled it across the tiny backs of
his knuckles as we drove so that it blurred into motion
and we still hadnt reached yaqui buoy yet were still just
picking through the boneyard they call it the rolling
boneyard all the abandoned cars people still sneak back
over the border at night to scavenge and you can see them
from the road sometimes but not because theyre careless
but because theyre running and god naitche was in love
with them always just outside the anthropologists spot-
lights always just ahead of the four wheel drive trucks
fishtailing behind them always screaming and shooting
those wooden arrows back at the trucks not because they
could bring the trucks down but because they could slow
them because no anthropologist can resist easing off the
pedal to pick through the mud for an arrow especially if
it has some clan crest (they think we have crests) or is
sheathed in say a bumpersticker which they can take back
to the lab and peel with forceps and preserve under glass
with the appropriate number so that anybody who wants to
know if the raiders as theyre called if the raiders of
whatever year supported republicans or were gone fishin
or would rather be smoking kinnikinnick or whatever
bumpersticker was easiest to steal from the store that
season and once the second night closer to the territories one of them stood up into our headlights in an
elaborate headdress and stared at us until he saw we were
indian and then at the last second jumped straight up

plucking our hood ornament off on the way to pin it to
the stars and it was too dark to see if he ever landed or
not with his water pumps and compressors and tie rods
slung in a seatcover over his shoulder but naitche watched
out the back window until he fell asleep like that and i
want it not to be like this for him sitting in the car in
the daytime rolling the token across the tiny backs of
his knuckles until it blurs into the image of a father
for him maybe quetzalcoatl the plumy god the feathered
serpent coiled and jumping up into the night with auto-
motive loot and coming down with me at the rodeo grounds
careful to take all the shock of reentry himself which
shakes blood from his nose onto my chest this is what he
does his blood can bring you back to life it can fall on
old bones in a neat line like the finger holes of a flute
and the night will fill with syrupy rich music not
screaming not sirens not ambulances not chanting and
drums and one cow deep in the showbarn lowing in unnatural birth because there is no unnatural birth are you
listening there is no unnatural birth theres only miracles
one ~~god~~ man running headlong from his last name to his
first down the milky white sterile halls of the hospital
youve guessed by now dont lie and then taking the first
empty bed there is for us because when the plumy god the
feathered serpent when he turns everything around backwards so that instead of making the woman the swan *he*
changes into one and you love him for that but you hate
him too for jumping over the car that night instead of
leaning into the window either side for his son or his

milk maid

       or *mary* to the red catholics or *lady* or *madonna*
or a creamy white homogenized statue standing above an
almond brown city the blue veins in her pale breast
poisoning her fatherless child the anasazis immaculate
reconception the little girl on the television set her
insides full of powdery tablets to absorb the dairy only
they were too good they absorbed everything until she
was like the black beetles her and thomas used to touch
with twigs in what used to be oklahoma so that their hard
backs would cave in and flake away like ashes and there
collected at the bottom of their abdomens would be this
white powder like condensed milk only they thought it
was poison (it was) and sometimes it made him throw up
just looking at how *wrong* it was to be dry like that

inside a body and they never could eat the powdered sugar
tart candy michael stole from the convenience store
because it reminded them too much of touching the bugs of
seeing into the bugs how the bugs didnt *care* if their
backs flaked off and after enough shoots and enough cups
of milk the girl started feeling like the beetles like
she was full of poison of white powder and didnt care
either was just crawling across the green grass on the
back side of the television screen and smiling somehow
the whole time maybe because the morning star was always
rising in those commercials no matter the season the
director said it was authentic it was tribal it was
necessary and she knew who it was or what (a hood ornament) and she would just watch it and pull the bleached
white robe tighter around her shoulders and she never
knew it was real all that grass all that grass*land* until
her and naitche turned away from yaqui buoy the tragedy
there the car wedged over him thirty yards into america
the ihs ambulance careening there trying to beat the
american ambulance because in no mans land its first
come first serve finders keepers all that a race everytime
but she never knew there was so much grass until she
turned the car off at the top of the hill and pulled her
son to her so he wouldnt try to count each individual
blade so a part of him wouldnt be there forever but it
was maybe too late already maybe he was already a part of
it always had been and after that they drove only at
night to protect him and she let him read the pamphlets
the anasazi had given them about the boneyard the junkyard
the *salvage* yard the remains of the parade the legend
that from all these leftover rusting parts one truck was
going to come together one red one white truck america
wanted but it was too fast for america too uncatchable
and that was what the raiders were looking for and he
looked at me like he was going to ask me about it about
*some*thing maybe the token maybe the anasazi hearing the
car from america seconds too late and i held my breath
for miles looking straight ahead and when i opened my
mouth powdered milk coughed down onto the sloped front
of my shirt and he touched it like it was still rising
from a broken can that had rolled off the top shelf of
the grocery store and then he put it to his tongue and i
looked away'

why don't you grow your hair like a real Indian?

because i'm not.

A Good Day to Die Again

PINK EYE was all the rage. It started in the backrooms and bathrooms of all the bars, the dirty places IHS had left it, because they know Indians. It was supposed to help us. This was back in the days of the skin test, back when the standard for being Indian was nipple color, because you can't fake that, not with a prosthetic, not with a rub-on pigment. But not everyone wanted to be Indian bad enough to raise their shirt at the door. So IHS gave us pink eye, retroengineered it from the smallpox America was supposed to still have, was supposed to be wafting over the border at us for stealing back the Great Plains then trying to burn them down. Now in their history books they call it a ritual cleansing, the Fire, but it was still just a cigarette arcing forever out a car window.

And the smallpox never came.

Instead America made us bargains for bulk razor blades, gave them away with lighters, taught us to carry them in the brittle plastic sheaths of our cigarette packs along with the pictures we could never throw away.

The year after the parade twenty percent of the population was floating dead in bathtubs. Because the party was winding down. But then the nurses and staff of IHS started showing up in the bars, squinting like moles, leaving tiny glass vials in the ashtrays and tip jars. At first nobody noticed—everybody was already hung over anyway, eyes bloodshot—but then it didn't go away, and only Indians had it. Instead of untucking your shirt at the door, now, you just looked into their eyes, smiled. If you were Indian. If you hadn't been vaccinated. But there are ways. There are always ways.

I stayed up until dawn transcribing Cat Stand's sentence, then drawing lines from her to Denim Horse, to Back Iron, to LP Deal, and from LP Deal to Mary Boy, and then to Owen82 and Bacteen. And from Bacteen to Nickel Eye.

My pencil trembled on the paper.

'So how was America?' Eddie Dial asked, biting his lower lip. We were at the table by lane 15, my eyes Indian red behind the sunglasses. I felt like Mary Boy, watching Fool's Hip under glass, from a distance. But it can all rush up to you so fast—just a phone, ringing, ringing.

LP Deal answered when no one else would, and it was for a Miss Dick. The name I'd given the hotline. I turned away, blew smoke into the fan of Denim Horse's ball return, but LP Deal was staring right at me.

'This a real call?' he asked finally, into the receiver, and then said there was no Dick here, no, and I closed my eyes in appreciation, the smoke coming back at me all at once.

'So?' Eddie Dial asked, and I just shook my head. His face was scratched on one side, and I wanted to take pictures, see if the pattern matched his nails, or Back Iron's long ones, or Denim Horse, still living that game. Or what.

'Who did that?' I asked.

He took my cigarette, inhaled hard. 'Miss America,' he said.

Courtney Peltdowne looked up when he said it. Eddie Dial blew smoke in her general direction. She had one of LP Deal's notebooks open behind her beauty magazine. We all knew it. If Back Iron had been there we could have made a show out of pretending not to notice, but he was nowhere. A postcard now, overnight, flaunting the truck. That day the postal trains were fat with him, too, thirty thousand postcards and more, all addressed *Washington DC.* They were supposed to overload the system. In the animated section of the six o'clock news, the streets and gutters of DC ran red with it. And when it clotted, God, but that was the night after tomorrow, the next installment.

My eyes were also red from crying.

This was the day Cat Stand bowled 287, Naitche sitting at her table backwards, watching the arcade. It was deserted. Even LP Deal was skirting it. It was more than the sunglasses: Fool's Hip was different now. The lines I drew weren't long enough; LP Deal was wearing locker keys pinned to his coveralls. He said the toilet had been spitting them back up. They rattled as he swept and I didn't eat anything all day. Denim Horse had two tourists for lunch. Nickel Eye had beer. It was on the house.

The person screaming on the inside was me. The one not calling you to swoop in with a tribal helicopter used to be Special Agent Chassis Jones. But she knew you were coming. That Back Iron's postcard would bring you. That you would see her blonde hair and Indian eyes and she would nod a private nod to the locker where this folder is going to be, this report, and if she brushed up against you in the concession line it would be accidental, not a plea, but she won't show anything on her face, and you won't either. Or, she won't if you don't until you do.

When they ask why I came here, tell them it was to get my gun. And don't say that I fell in love. Tell them instead about

Smudge, the medicine man for the Council, standing all that day
in the shadow of Red Dawn. He had white feathers at his elbows
and the tops of his boots, and his face was painted glossy black.
At six o'clock exactly, the glass door still swinging from Mary
Boy's slow fade into dusk, a black-lipped coyote padded into Fool's
Hip, and I could no longer breathe people air. Nickel Eye wasn't
at his place at the bar. Cat Stand's ball slammed into the gutter.
Denim Horse's box fan died, his hair falling all around him. I
stood but Eddie Dial guided me back down, and the coyote passed,
touching everything with its nose, cleansing it, cleansing it, leading Smudge out in a complicated dance that would have taken
days to unfold.

He didn't take my wig off like I thought he would, either. Or
my sunglasses. But still I had to check them, in the bathroom where
no one could see. Through the open window I could hear Mary
Boy's throaty vespers. The beauty magazine was on the sill, too.
Where Courtney Peltdowne had been listening. I sat in her place
until it was over, watching Mary Boy raise his knees with the words,
eyes closed behind his sunglasses, the stray cat dancing behind him,
and asked on the metal wall if this is how it all starts, if this is how
it was for Enil Anderson and the rest, but then scratched his name
out, my nail file moving sometimes in a blur, sometimes not at all.

Miss America was a ghost by then. Number forty-one. I didn't
even look for her.

The next morning Mary Boy was wearing his *pan-indian* apron,
which meant he was cooking. The hard scent of buffalo drifted
over the lanes and down the alleys. Earlier, LP Deal had been
singing—I had heard him through the mail slot with Courtney
Peltdowne, dawn washing up red behind us—but now he was
bent over the markers, rolling the arrowheads up carefully, lining
them up for the Councilmen.

Tonight there was going to be a play.

It was the stage production of *Susannah of the Mounties*, the
players were professional nomads. The posters called the show a

Dramatic Reversion, and in the background of the words was a photograph the first maintenance man at Fool's Hip had taken years ago, looking north. You could still see the tipi rings in the yellow grass. I looked to the ceiling for the first time, my throat pale and vulnerable.

'You speak Lakota?' a tourist asked Nickel Eye across the pit. He looked to her, parted his lips in a dry smile.

'Speak it?' he said. 'Hell, Miss, I don't even *listen* to it.'

When the tourist sat down with me in the line for Denim Horse she wouldn't say anything.

'Are you dead?' I asked her, and she turned her head slowly to me.

Yes.

Nickel Eye had told her his dad had been so Indian he could hear the deers' antlers mineralizing. It was something about how sound traveled after the first snow. It was why he hunted blindfolded, to be fair.

'Why didn't he wear clothes, though?' she asked, finishing his joke like it was gospel—serious—and I stepped cleanly out of line, followed Courtney Peltdowne up and down the length of Fool's Hip. It was a sensuous circuit; LP Deal's coveralls were a tent, blown over. Finally he approached with tickets in hand, fawning, talking first into his wrist then remembering, looking up to her (she was taller than him). The tickets were for the play that night. They had been everywhere when Fool's Hip opened—tucked into the screens of the video games, layered into the toilet paper, rolled into the thumbholes of balls. The players had been here last night, drumming up an audience.

'No,' she said to him, looking to Denim Horse the whole time, 'sorry.'

LP Deal tilted his head back to drain the rejection down his throat, and when Courtney Peltdowne was past I touched the tickets still clutched in his hand, became a rustling on his tape of that day, and said I would go with him. I would be honored.

'There's a new piece, tonight,' he said, showing me the tickets in his palm. It was Make Him Dance. Owen82 had written it, mailed it into the contest months and months and months ago. The ticket billed it as one of the lost episodes, originally left on the cutting room floor. We were all supposed to play along, had been playing along already for years, the real *Susannah* being replaced show by show, performance by performance. Other lost episodes were The Latterday Coup Machine, There Is No Water, Pale Young Four Toes, The Unphallic Tale of the Woodpecker, Exit the Warrior. They were standard fare in elementary, even— the young Junior from The Unphallic Woodpecker, killing birds for his grandmother because they're drilling holes into her attic, then finally realizing it was his *grand*mother who moved in on the woodpeckers; that he was the American here. In elementary school his suicide is off-stage, though, in the footnotes. You don't see it as it is until you're old enough and it's too late.

But Make Him Dance. That was going to be Denim Horse after that last game. It had to be. Peeling his jersey, stepping into the feathered boots.

What LP Deal wanted from it was answers. To walk up on Owen82 dead in the ditch and know who did it. I think even then Mary Boy thought it might have been him, LP Deal. Standing over Owen82 with the smoking gun. Maybe he hired him that day just to keep him there. Or maybe he did it himself.

But that's his investigation.

Mine is Nickel Eye.

I keep having to say it, though.

The night before Special Agent Chassis Jones sat in the front row of *Susannah of the Mounties* with a custodian half her age, she had that dream again about Nickel Eye—standing kneedeep in the field of Indian hair, him holding her hand. I had been awake, though, out at the crumbling edge of the parking lot of Broken Arrow (again), so maybe it doesn't count. Naitche had led me out there. Well. His dim form had walked past my window, and I had followed.

He was talking to somebody out there. I could smell them.

Miss America?

Back Iron?

Gauche?

And we didn't need tickets for *Susannah* after all. Mary Boy paid for the show with food, and they performed it down at the end of the lanes, innertubes wrapped around their feet so they wouldn't slip on the waxed lanes. We all helped unfold the chairs that afternoon, line them up, and when the bus came from America that afternoon, we turned the lights off and pretended to be closed. Because this was an Indian thing; flashbulbs would frighten the players up into the ball returns of Fool's Hip, leave us all sitting there, unsure whether it was part of the show or not. And I fully expected Back Iron to lower himself hand over hand into the game Make Him Dance was going to be. He would be wearing the same wig as in the postcard; he would be playing Denim Horse.

I was wrong.

The players entered through the open bathroom window two hours before the show, each dipping his tongue in the butter bowl of water we left there. One of them I remembered from high school; his name had been OD. The short muscles of his eyes still twitched with it, but he had an appetite now, they all did. And Miss America was with them, the newest, most temporary member.

'Thar she blows,' Nickel Eye said, winking at me.

'Who?' I said, lowering my sunglasses; pretending.

Nickel Eye laughed.

Miss America was wearing a string bikini, stars and stripes. Her thick braids sloped down over her thick breasts. Her make-up was all worn off, too. I didn't ask.

'Guess she found her niche,' Nickel Eye was saying behind me, talking slow.

'...along with everybody else,' Eddie Dial said back, coughing into his hand, his smile crackling the scabs of his face.

Miss America. *Not* number forty-one. Not the same, at least. She touched my hair as she passed, her hand slow, rising from a dream.

Beside me Nickel Eye rotated his shoulders around his beer, lowered his head into his shoulders, and adjusted his olive green jacket so that he disappeared, even though he was the only olive green thing in the place.

Where he had been standing was Cat Stand. I nodded yes to her, though I didn't know the question. Last night I hadn't had my wig on at the laundromat. I was trying to tell her that I was the same person anyway, maybe. She had her arm draped over Naitche. He was staring at Miss America, at OD, at Eberhard and the one calling himself Longfellow, and probably seeing in the way they stood the shape of the whole play, even though it was improvised everytime.

I was scared of him and I wanted to hold him in my lap both, stroke his glossy hair under the hot lights. In the Bacteen story on KORL coming back from America, I had kept wanting to tell Bacteen that he was never leaving the truck, that Coyote was just changing the backdrop outside the window, that the rear wheels of the truck were on rollers, and the rollers were connected to gears, and the gears were rolling all that history past. But then he hunched his head into his shoulders and stepped into it.

In the pit, all the machines were going

CAT
CAT
CAT
CAT
CAT
LPD
LPD
LPD
LPD
LPD
LPD
LPD
LPD
lpd
b.p

We ate buffalo until our chins were shiny, and sometime before the show, Longfellow put on white feathers like Smudge, stood like a cigar-store Indian by the door until everyone was uncomfortable. Miss America led him away, to the folding chairs he would rise from. Instead of a prologue, LP Deal swept out in the spotlight, nodded to us like *what?*, then lowered his ear to the hardwood, for the Councilmen, for the AllSkin Tournament.

He stood nodding, nodding, and we exploded into applause, I don't know why. Even Mary Boy. Even Courtney Peltdowne.

LP Deal sat back down by me. His coveralls were still heated from the attention.

The first act was more like a newsreel: some Mister X stealing into the reliquary at Pine Ridge, driving the truck out. No words, no lines, just action. From the rafters someone applauded and it was too dark but it was Back Iron. He was becoming part of it now—his image captured in the hologram, his silhouette on stage. There wasn't enough left of him to sit with us anymore. He was legend.

I squeezed LP Deal's hand.

The second episode was a complete replay of the Indian Wars. Miss America carried the tiles across stage: *scene 1, scene 1 again, another scene 1, scene one, one scene.* The bodies stacked up so high she had to get a running start.

It all ended here, at Fool's Hip.

LP Deal squeezed my hand back.

When the show was over, in his empty seat there would be a folded packet of paper for me. A self-portrait, 'Blue Moons.' The things he couldn't say. There would be two grainy photographs rolled in with it too. That was all later, though, fanned out on a bedspread at Broken Arrow. First, the show—the image of LP Deal holding his wrist down the alley, waiting for Owen82. To record him.

I held my hand out with him, so the players wouldn't know they were being bootlegged, and three chairs down Mary Boy held his arm out too, Jesus sweating blood on his arm, and then everyone in the front row was reaching downlane, for the show, and when I looked over at LP Deal I saw for the first time that half of his ear was gone, scraped off.

To mark the new episode, Fool's Hip faded to black for a few close moments, then came back. Nothing would ever be the same again.

MAKE HIM DANCE

A prairie night, a campfire, a domino mask. Tonto
is leaned back on his bedroll, staring over his
coffee at the Lone Ranger.

A horse stamps, blows.

Tonto stares, drinks.

'So this is how it is,' he says.

The Lone Ranger doesn't reply, doesn't even move.

Tonto's face is streaked black across the
cheeks.

Nobody says kimosabe.

Their fire is buffalo chips, their camp cloy-
ing. An unexplained urgency.

Suddenly Tonto turns his head to the darkness.
It's empty, quiet, and then a girl steps out.
'I didn't hear you,' he says.
She shrugs. Her shoes are in her hands.
'Can I?' she says, looking down at a saddle
propped up as a backrest.
'Free country,' Tonto says. But he's smiling.
The girl sits down.
'You don't talk the same,' she says.
'Sit um down?' Tonto tries, handing her his
cup.
She looks off. The horse stamps again, blows.
'Silver?' she asks.
'More like white.'
And now the Lone Ranger's gloved hand
twitches. Like a wave. The girl waves back, her
fingertips drumming the ground too.
'You even wear that at night?' she asks him—
the mask—and reaches across the fire to touch it.
Or his cheek. But Tonto shakes his head no.
'All these strong, silent types,' she says.
Tonto has his cup again.
'I used to listen to you, you know,' she says.
'On the radio.'
Tonto narrows his eyes at her.
'The *radio*,' she says, with her whole mouth,
then leans over, touching her ear to the ground
for *listen*, looking at him with a question mark.
He can see down her bodice, now.
'Rad-ee-o,' he says.
'But it was real, too,' she says. 'Like I
always thought there was this third horse running
behind you—both of you—with like a boom, a *mic*,
tied to its saddle horn...'
Tonto looks out to the horses, then jerks back
when the Lone Ranger's leg spasms. The rowel of
the spur digs into the packed dirt.
'He alright?' the girl asks.
'Hard day,' Tonto says.

'Guess so,' she says, then touches her own face for him, Tonto, like he's got something there.

'Thanks,' Tonto says, and moves his cup to the other hand, touches his fingertip to his cheek like she is.

It just makes it worse, though.

Now his war paint isn't symmetrical.

He looks at his hand, at her. With a question mark.

Before she can answer, though, the Lone Ranger speaks: 'When the chips are down, Tonto, well, sir, now that's when the buffalo's empty.'

His voice is mechanical.

'Got ya,' Tonto says, fingershooting him across the fire.

The girl is looking at both of them now.

She touches the Lone Ranger's boot with her foot. It rotates without the leg. Tonto closes his eyes, opens them.

'Hard day?' she says.

'Miners,' Tonto says. 'A stagecoach.'

She's still staring at him.

He smiles. 'I can hear them coming from miles away, you know.'

She nods.

Tonto rubs his eye, smearing the paint. Staring at nothing, the emptied coffee cup hooked on his finger, his hand on his knee, his leg propped.

'You shouldn't drink so much,' she says.

'I don't like to sleep out here,' Tonto says.

'But you're...Indian.'

Tonto smiles, nods.

The sky yawns above him.

'When the chips are—' the Lone Ranger starts to say again, but Tonto stomps his foot on the ground.

'*Hi-ho Silver!*' the Lone Ranger says instead, raising one gloved hand above his head.

'That really him?' the girl asks.

Tonto nods, watches her.

'Want some more?' he asks finally, swirling the grounds in the bottom of his cup.

The girl nods, then flinches when he braces himself to stand.

'It's okay,' he tells her, but keeps both hands up as he backs into the darkness. A horse whinnies. Supplies touch each other with a tin sound, muffled by leather. This is 1890. Tonto walks back into camp with a bag labeled COFFEE. He tosses it down onto the Lone Ranger's lap. The Lone Ranger stares at him. Tonto stares back.

'It's okay, really,' the girl says, 'I can come—' but Tonto shushes her.

'*Coffee*,' he says. To the Lone Ranger.

But the Lone Ranger just sits there.

Tonto shakes his head.

'This always happens,' he says.

The girl doesn't ask what.

A horse stamps just past the firelight and a boom lowers over them. They both see it.

'Shh,' Tonto almost says, holding a black finger over his lips.

'So...,' the girl says, ' a stagecoach...' and Tonto nods, rolls his hand in the Indian signal for more, cover him, and as she recounts the episode he creeps over behind the Lone Ranger, opens a panel in the back of the denim shirt.

The girl catches her breath.

Tonto stares at her, red and green lights blinking off his face.

She closes her eyes, continues: '...and he was on the rocks like that. *Dry gulch!* Sam yelled—I think that was his name—but it was too late...'

Tonto smiles around the knife in his teeth.

His hands are deep in the Lone Ranger's back.

The black paint is grease.

The girl is crying down the back of her throat
and talking around it.

'Okay,' Tonto says to her, holding his palm
out.

She trails off, leaving someone midair.

Tonto closes the panel, coughs to cover the
click.

'Now,' he says, walking back to the fire,
looking down at the Lone Ranger, 'coffee.'

The Lone Ranger's face snaps up. The domino
mask. All the fringe.

'Coffee?' he asks, his voice deep and heroic.

'More like it,' Tonto says.

He squats down on his haunches.

'I always thought you sat like that,' the girl
says.

She sits down like him, like a little girl,
and before them the Lone Ranger stands, dragging
his rotated boot, and goes through the motions of
coffee.

'Delicious,' the girl says when it's done,
holding her cup with both hands.

Tonto nods, blowing steam off his own, never
looking away.

The Lone Ranger tips his crisp white hat to
him, says ma'am to the girl.

In her cup is a silver bullet. She spits it
into her palm.

'Oh,' she says.

She looks to Tonto.

'It's real,' he says, 'that part.'

'Hi-ho Si—' the Lone Ranger starts, but Tonto
slaps the ground with his palm, stopping him mid-
sentence, his arm on the way up.

The rowels of one of his spurs is left spinning.

Tonto pinches the bridge of his nose hard.

The girl closes her hand around the bullet,
holds it close to her chest.

'Thank you,' she says, then looks up to the Lone Ranger, standing over her. Behind him one of the horses drums its hoof on the ground and the Lone Ranger moves the arm by his side, straightening it out behind him.

Again; again.

The girl smiles, sweeping her eyes across the dark prairie to see who might be watching.

Tonto shakes his head, leans back against his bedroll.

'What is it already?' he says, not quite grinning around his cup, and, her voice small like a question, she says it, and the night pares itself back down again, to a campfire, a domino mask, two white eyes looking out of it in terror.

cortez (my father's armor)
Picture a boy and he's running. Everything washed out like a memory: grass the color of beer; his house stained with it.

He swings onto the porch and lets the blind dog smell him.

In the living room the horizontal hold on the television is shot, and the picture rolls up and up like smoke and he watches it, breathing hard.

Behind him the blind dog has its nose to the screen door, its marbled eyes dry, unblinking.

He closes the door on them but it won't: the hinges have been kicked in. There's rawhide there now, tied to something deep in the modular wall and then to the screws in the door, backed out halfway, just far enough to tie to.

Is this how the old Indians did it?

He lifts the door into its rectangle of light, lines the deadbolt up.

The house is quiet; wrong.

He won't ever forget this.

In the thick amber curtains, backlit by the sun, is a shape, a form, a man.

Neither of them moves.

Neither of them says anything.

From the back of the house—his mother's room—the floor creaks; a footstep.

He turns to it, opens his mouth, then turns back to the shape.

Father.

He's home.

Using the leg of the kitchen table that comes off, he lifts the curtain gauze away, falls back into the couch swinging.

It's a suit of armor; a husk.

He narrows his eyes at it, doesn't say *Dad*. Hasn't ever seen him really, just heard him when he comes through. Seen the silver cans when he's gone, accepted the gifts he leaves on the coffee table, the kitchen counter. Behind the curtains.

The commercial on the television is a milk commercial, that girl. He turns it off after touching her face with his finger—a kiss—then stands before the armor, looking up.

It's golden, powerful. The gift this time.

He smiles, looks down the hall.

Thank you. It's exactly.

Touching it with his fingertips, he's Incan.

Holding it around the waist, the side of his face pressed to its stomach, he doesn't know what he is.

He lowers it to the carpet gently, as if it could shatter. Imagines his father dragging it across three states for him, day and night. No, wearing it. Looking down at his poker cards and then up at the conquistadors sitting around the table with him, taking them for everything they have.

He opens the face part and it's empty.

He rolls it over and the back opens up.

He puts in one leg, then the next, and it comes apart at the waist. Leaving just the breastplate part.

He crawls in anyway, into the fetal position, and closes his eyes, wakes hours later, the metal the same temperature as his body.

People are screaming around him.

His mother and father, spilled out of the bedroom. Larger than the bedroom.

They haven't seen him.

Glass crashes; the rest of the legs come off the kitchen table.

Eyes closed or open it doesn't matter.

And the words are all the same.

He feels the armored legs get kicked away, into the halfwall between the kitchen and the living room.

They still haven't seen him.

Are still screaming.

Mother; Father; Dad.

If he cries it doesn't matter. As long as he's quiet. He pulls his ears down into his shoulders when they talk about him. Is running again.

Out the opposite armhole he can see the refrigerator open finally, the beer pour out.

It's almost over.

All that's left is his mother, thrown against the back door, then his father's legs leaving by the back door, closing it on his mother's hair. Her arms won't reach the knob, either.

They never see him. That's the thing.

An hour later the front door crashes in again, the rawhide hinges giving because the deadbolt won't.

Dad.

His mother looks up at him, and they stare, and then she stands with a tearing sound, scalping herself, her hair locked in the back door, blood trailing down her face, and his father kneels breathing by the breastplate, unhooks the helmet, watching her all the time, and puts it on, says something from its confines, then crashes into the thin wall of the living room four times headfirst, exploding out into the night.

His mother is unconscious by the time he calls the ambulance, his father three states away.

They never see him.

vd (my mother's name)

Picture a boy and he's running. All the cars of the parking lot nosed up to the community center like horses, hunched away from the cold; still steaming.

Inside is a pandance.

He stands at the door, breathing hard.

In front of him is an old man in a red bandanna and a folding chair. Ninety-two years of sunlight folded into the skin of his face, eyes cloudy from it.

'Yeah?' the old man says, then stamps the boy's hand Indian, ushers him in.

His mother is here. That's what he heard, why he was running in the heavy armor.

He doesn't say her name, though. Knows better.

And no one can see his armor.

Mother.

He looks for her through slits in the visor, his eyes narrowed, but she's every woman walking by with a drink held near her collarbone, a black wig; a certain sadness.

Six times he sees her, and six times he follows, trying hard to bend his knees like everyone else, to not look mechanical. But that only makes it worse.

The drum circles he stumbles into pause until he leaves, then match his footsteps, making them larger.

A bundle of spent fancydancers hears him coming, starts pointing to him with their chins, smiling through their feathers.

He locks his arms and elbows when they touch him, so they carry him through the crowd at shoulder-level, passing him from dancer to dancer, bird to bird, and at their cooler they tilt him back, pour beer into his helmet; laugh.

Their names are jokes, looted from fashion magazines and movie reviews.

He remembers every one of them.

Up in the metal rafters ten year olds are smoking, their ash settling on the people below, coloring them grey and immaterial.

The boy smiles.

Staggers from the dancers. First just away, then against the bleachers: up, up. As high as he can get.

The children in the rafters are drawn to his armor.

They pass him a cigarette, point with their eyes to the next target, the tall dancer in dyed blue feathers.

Insert here one cigarette, one finger, one tap; a breath of ash.

Minutes later the dancer looks up into the darkness and the children all become rusted iron, just part of the structure. Still though, an arrow sails up between them, punctures the roof. Fiberglass spins down, all the smoke in the place rushing past it at once.

The bow clatters to the ground, the dancer ~~walking~~ striding away from it. Towards the wooden stands on the opposite side. Towards a woman. Her.

She's made of brown paper.

Everytime he stands in line at a grocery store now he thinks of that. Brown paper and black silk.

VD.

He rolls his helmet off his head to see her better. To warn her. All the children turn to watch her. It's like watching birds watch a cat.

One of them stands as the dancer parts the cluster of people just below her.

The boy is breathing hard now.

He tries to run down the bleachers, but will never make it. Instead he steps out of the leg armor, takes the hands the children are offering him, but the breastplate is too heavy for them.

'C'mon,' they say, biting cigarettes in half; coughing black.

And so he takes the breastplate off, swings arm over arm four times, as much as he's got. After that he just hangs naked from an I-beam.

Miles below, everyone is singing at once together, the Love Song of Nathaniel Hybird, a favorite this year.

His mother is tapping her foot with it, too. Looking at him like it means something.

The song?

Her foot?

Mom. Mother.

Even if he had a voice.

Even if he could swing across the rafters to her.

Even if she was really looking at him. Saying goodbye.

He lets go with his fingers, pads into the bleachers, taking the fall at all four points, the wooden seat rushing up at his face; trembling. With sound.

He smiles, lowers his head to it, his ear, to listen to the code she's tapping out with her foot. To pick her footstep out from all the rest.

When he stands, though, she's gone. Everyone is.

All that's left is the breastplate.

He walks down to it, and instead of lifting it over his head, crawls into it like a turtle and pokes his head out the neckhole, wearing it backwards; looking both ways slowly. He crawls like that out the door, each step testing the ground, taking him that much farther away.

On the back of his hand in red ink is *in dio*—in god.

It's a message from her.

He retraces it every night for months.

naitche (my inner papoose)

Picture a boy and he's running. The Territories set up around him like dominoes, a house of cards; a labyrinth.

Over the years his copper shell has weathered down to faded tan coveralls.

His left side is on fire, too. He clutches it, slows to a walk, picks through Broken Leg sober. It's the worse way. One of the prairie dogs rises from its hole with a shiny pistol, motioning the boy who's not anymore on.

Keep it moving, keep it moving.

He does, one foot after the other, one shoe then the next, and that night he understands why you make campfires when you don't really need them: to have something in the center, a focus. Without it you're looking out into the darkness all the time. Over your shoulder.

He talks to himself out loud in two voices, to fool anybody listening, and then in the morning almost forgets which he is, was, whatever.

By late afternoon he sees it, sitting squat and rectangular on the horizon. All bricks and paint and bad ideas.

It's like the booth he's been in for two years, just bigger, and on its side.

He approaches on the road.

A coyote pads away grinning.

He opens his mouth to yell to it, *say* something, but his voice is gone.

There by the road is a man.

The boy who isn't approaches walking sideways, never looking directly in the ditch, but then he does, and has to stand over him: it.

The man's eyes are marbled grey, the skin around them pale from wearing sunglasses.

On his shirt is a whistle.

Under the whistle is a strip of paper.

The boy shakes his head no, no, then looks fast to the fast road behind him, but it's empty. But he watches it, breathing hard.

The first thing he picks up is the gun. So the prairie dogs won't get it, make an army; steal the Territories back.

The second thing is the note.

The third is the whistle.

The whistle he puts in his mouth and breathes through; blows through. It's shrill and loud and no birds answer, no Warriors rise from the ground to run bleachers. Except him, dancing from foot to foot in the cold, staring at the sun, trying to fold it all into his face too, his eyes, so he won't have to see this; be here.

The note is decayed by the wind already.

On the front side it says

> *had life rotten*
> *nod at the rifle.*

It's Algonquin for goodbye.

He eats it, swallows just as the door of the place opens, the pins crashing over the grass to him.

The last thing he does is throw the gun back down.

But it's too late for that.

He doesn't look up, instead stands in place and backs into himself, until he's staring out of the pit at his mother again. But she has her back to him. Her hair like black silk, her form perfect, advancing for him in stages, in frames, until her release. She holds it, holds it, and then the whole place comes crashing down when her ball reaches the end of the alley, opening up a hole. Somebody stepping through.

Red Dawn

PINK EYE was all the rage. All the Councilmen had it for the tournament. They were so Indian the anthropologists launched themselves past with catapults, shutters clicking. It was like a plague of locusts. They didn't even look up, though, didn't even smile. The way they held their shoulders said they'd seen it all before, but they hadn't. Not Fool's Hip anyway.

Nickel Eye was standing beside me, nursing a toothpick.

He named them as they pulled in: Double Clutch, the Lumbee mechanic; Gooseneck, the onetime trucker; Big Hair, mother of none, Lead Foot, the occasional smuggler; Sister Venetia, the blind one out of Thermal Illinois; Last Success, the misplaced Yankton;

Bat Lashes, the ex-actress.

'Seven,' I said. Like the sins.

LP Deal ran past, stooping over for rocks to sling at the flying anthropologists, and Nickel Eye handed him a metal helmet. LP Deal took it in stride, threw so hard the forehead of his golden helmet nearly kissed the caliche of the parking lot, but it was just a gesture: they had only been within range for as long as it took the Councilmen to wait out their dust cloud, open the doors of their long cars, and walk across the parking lot into Fool's Hip.

Mary Boy was holding the door open for them, his mirrored shades impervious to the thousand tiny suns of the anthropologists' cameras. Sister Venetia ran her hand over the raised skin of his tattoo, then tasted her fingertips. Double Clutch handed his equipment bag to LP Deal. Lead Foot memorized the parking lot, already mapping a getaway. Gooseneck shook Nickel Eye's hand, then touched my hair like Last Success was elbowing him to. I lifted my chin away, though, watched the anthropologists landing a quarter mile off, the parachutes on the backs of their chairs billowing over Broken Leg.

'Don't let them build anything there,' Nickel Eye said.

I might have been holding his hand then, I don't know.

He kept looking to the roof.

'What?' I asked.

'Nothing,' he said.

The anthropologists had been that high, though. Meaning there are pictures of it all somewhere; proof. The anthropologists carried it back to America for us—breaking their chairs down into go-carts and driving fast for the border, leaving one of their kind with his leg in a hole, the prairie-dog people already working on it.

'Your eyes,' Nickel Eye said then, tapping his own.

I had my sunglasses off.

My eyes.

The anthropologist screamed.

Nickel Eye raised his hand; mine was around it, attached somehow. *Hand*cuffed. My handcuffs. From the locker at the station.

He formed my fingers into a pistol, lined up on the khaki shirt, made the sound with his mouth.

The anthropologist fell over, shot.

Nickel Eye blew smoke from under my fingernail.

Soon I was the only one out there. And both my hands were cuffed together.

I approached the slumped anthropologist, touched him with the toe of my shoe. He groaned. In his utility belt was a survival kit in molded plastic, like a Halloween costume. I toed it out, lost it down another hole and dived down after it, leading with both hands, the chain between them flashing.

In the hole were two things: the kit and my pistol.

I brought them both up.

Nickel Eye had told me this somehow. That my pistol would be here. That I could go now.

But I didn't.

The kit was up-to-date, too. Had the standard issue eye drops that were supposed to allow the stranded anthropologist to walk back to America unmolested. The eye drops were red dye suspended in a saline solution.

There are ways, I said to myself, face tilted back for the drops. There are always ways.

I walked into Fool's Hip crying blood. Just another Indian.

The two photographs LP Deal had left in the seat with his packet of papers were of upper arms. One his, one Naitche's. On each there were bruise-colored fingernail impressions—a line of half moons, curved like the lunar track, even: rising, rising, falling; four stages, eight, a circle. A story in pictures.

The idea, I think, was that just as VD had grabbed his arm once, Cat Stand was grabbing Naitche's.

It was a third-party neglect report, form 2299A.

And he had turned it in to the proper authorities.

And there was nothing I could do with it.

LP Deal stopped mopping to mark my entrance. It was like the play was still going on. Like we had all been conscripted as actors.

I avoided his eyes, walked mechanically past the concession stand, my wrists together in front of me, the chain in my palms.

On the table where I usually sat with Eddie Dial was a note: you had called again. On the payphone. For Miss Dick.

I closed my eyes, opened them. Should have known.

'What?' Eddie Dial asked, sitting down, shaking out one of my cigarettes.

He was the one person in the place who could tell Denim Horse from Back Iron if they didn't want you to. My folder was full of notes like this: *Eddie Dial knows Thomas from Michael; Cat ~~doesn't~~ didn't; NH remembers LP; LP remembers himself as NH; Mary Boy was on Owen82's side before he was Owen82; Bacteen never built his straw man.*

Your name was even on the note, Blue Plume.

I leaned back against the chair, the pistol cold against the small of my back.

Double Clutch slammed his twenty-pound ball into the pins. They exploded like birds. In the silence they left, Cat Stand and Denim Horse locked eyes across ten alleys.

Competition.

Double Clutch's ball was illegal, but he could throw it. And he was a Councilman anyway. Later he would pick up a spare with a bow and arrow he just had to hold his hand out for; Mary Boy brought a pitcher of beer himself. Double Clutch drained it down his throat without ever looking up, wiped his mouth with the back of his forearm, and smiled.

It was Cat Stand's turn.

He had heard about her.

She waited for his ball to come back, curled it up to her sternum with both hands, rested her chin on it.

Naitche was sitting at her scoring table. She looked back to him while she was lining up, and his head moved. You could hardly see it, but I was a regular by then; I could have heard the air rustle his hair if I'd needed to.

Even Nickel Eye turned to see what Cat Stand would do.

Mary Boy stepped out, his apron balled in his hand.

Courtney Peltdowne stood next to him, close.

Naitche smiled.

His mother's ball slammed into the back wall so hard the lights flickered. The clan bowlers rose as one, clapping their solemn claps. And Denim Horse. He nodded to her, smiled. Cat Stand turned away, closed her eyes. Her hand opening and closing.

I stood with Eddie Dial and the handcuffs rattled to the table.

There was a bobby pin in the keyhole.

I turned to the rafters in thanks.

This was the AllSkin tournament. This is the best way I know to describe it: fry bread, venison; molded plastic and golden beer; wooden pins with their necks ringed with color like ducks. The main prize was a white calf robe. It was supposed to be real, not bleached. Gooseneck made a show of unpinning one of the locker keys from LP Deal's coveralls, opening the locker, stuffing the robe in. Placing the key on the scoring table between Double Clutch and Cat Stand, then backing away. Maybe it was the same white robe she'd worn in the old commercials, handed down from person to person.

She didn't feed Naitche all day, either.

Maybe that was why LP Deal did it.

Second prize at the AllSkin Tournament was an all-paid weekend in the honeymoon suite of the Mayflower, courtesy of the Navajo. Eddie Dial said you didn't have to *marry* anybody, though, really—just an idea, a *slogan*, what every reservation needs if it wants to sell itself to America.

Nobody took us seriously.

It was supposed to be twelve words or less.

We're not savage anymore. Come see.

It's been nice, but now you have to leave.

We were taking care of it long before you, don't worry.

Yeah, it's a ~~dirty~~ mean place, but we like it.

Eddie Dial read them, pushed my napkin back at me. Looked away, blowing a thin stream of smoke. LP Deal was supposed to take it anyway. He'd probably make it into a haiku or something.

Eddie Dial shook his head no, though.

When his smoke cleared, LP Deal was sitting down at a table with Gooseneck and Venetia and Nickel Eye. Venetia was fanning a deck of cards from hand to hand.

'He hasn't been out of this place for... I don't know,' Eddie Dial said, '*ever.*'

He was right.

I thought of the chink in the wall, somebody stepping through. Not him.

Now Mary Boy was sitting down with them.

In LP Deal's notebook, this would show up as the Great Indian Poker Game in the Sky.

Naitche took all their cards in with a glance, then looked away, his lip trembling.

'What?' I started to say, but never got it out: Big Hair was leaning through the door.

She stood with a smile, her lipstick perfect.

Now I was shaking—my hand, my insides.

I took my cigarette back from Eddie Dial, hid behind it.

Her lipstick. She had been touching it up in her car, in the parking lot. When I had leaned back for the eyedrops.

She smiled at me.

The Great Indian Poker Game in the Sky was going on before her, LP Deal and Mary Boy and Venetia and Gooseneck and Nickel Eye sitting at all four corners of the table with cards stuck to the grease of their foreheads.

'Deal me in?' she said—Big Hair—and Venetia slid her a card off the top of the deck. Big Hair closed her eyes and lowered her forehead for it, and when she came up the card was a jewel under her column of hair and she was a queen, both hands flat on the table.

They all looked to her and waited.

Within ten minutes she'd ordered a sandwich for me. I peeled the extra tomatoes off and Eddie Dial ate them with salt.

I shook my head no to her—Big Hair—but it was too late. I'd been made. It didn't matter as what.

This would be my last day at Fool's Hip.

The third prize at the AllSkin tournament was local: Mary Boy and Nickel Eye and Longfellow had rigged it after the show the night before. It was a tape recording of a tribal elder ('Nikolai Sashmoon') recounting a Bacteen tale. The one the IHS had worked into circulation years ago, about vaccination.

I had watched them make it—Mary Boy holding LP Deal's wrist up to Nickel Eye like a microphone, Nickel Eye smoothing his hair down and trying to funnel all his gestures into verbs and nouns. LP Deal pretending none of this was happening, that nobody knew about his recording unit. Courtney Peltdowne whispering in his ear, her breath smoky like a bar.

All you had to do to win the tape was guess how many postcards had been mailed to DC in protest.

One, at least.

I knew about one.

I had signed it *Miss Dick*.

You were probably driving through Broken Leg about then. I had missed your call, but knew you were coming anyway: the postcards, the truck, the looted reliquary in Pine Ridge. A courtesy to the American government. An even trade for my Hotline-name.

I thought it would be different, though. That you would be professional.

Double Clutch's ball slammed into the back wall and I flinched.

We could all feel it rolling underground, back to Cat Stand.

Neither of them had missed a pin yet. The twenty-pound ball was weighing on Cat Stand, though. Her face was shiny with sweat. With each frame she was taking off another layer of flannel.

Later, Double Clutch would say she smelled like ice cream.

Later, Special Agent Chassis Jones would be gone.

You don't want to know where I'm writing this from. Who my roommate is.

There was no fourth prize.

Miss America was still in the bathroom, sitting on the sink, braiding a ribbon into her hair. Double Clutch's ball slammed into his sixth frame and Fool's Hip shuddered. Miss America closed her eyes, her fingers still moving, and white powder sifted down over us, balancing on every ceramic ledge, coating all the stainless steel.

'It's coming down,' she said, not really interested.

Already there were shafts of sunlight in the air, reflecting off the windshields of the Councilmen's cars into the side of Fool's Hip, *into* Fool's Hip. It was an egg, cracking open.

'You were good,' I told her.

She looked to me.

'Last night, I mean,' I said. 'With Tonto.'

She shrugged.

The main door was propped open, wouldn't close anymore. Through it we could hear Nickel Eye bidding, driving the pot up.

Miss America looked to him somehow.

'His father used to hunt deer with tennis balls,' I told her, repeating. 'His mother was Navajo, his father Diné.'

Miss America smiled.

'Is he…Him?' she asked.

I looked to the stall. After the ~~Roses~~ *are red* line, someone had carved *violence is blue*, and I didn't want to see the rest of the poem.

'I don't know what he is,' I told her.

My main suspect. A serial killer.

But after what Enil Anderson had done.

We won't hurt you, really, I told Eddie Dial in my head. For the honeymoon suite. It was just five words, though. I could do better.

Cat Stand's ball slammed into Fool's Hip.

Through the snow or ash or whatever it was Miss America said that she didn't know she was supposed to lose, did she—Cat Stand?

No, she didn't: Denim Horse was watching.

When I went out, she was down to her undershirt, and it was wet.

The twin glass doors opened behind me, all the dust in the air feinting towards them, and I didn't have to turn around to know it was you. Standing there framed by the light, taking your sunglasses off.

Courtney Peltdowne was sitting in front of me with a cigarette, her back to the game.

She narrowed her eyes against the sunlight. Had been there with Back Iron the first time we came, knew what to do: hold her wrists up, together, for the cuffs; smile. Say she'd been a bad, bad girl and arch her back away from the bench to show how much worse she could be, too.

I didn't have to turn around to know it was you, Blue Plume.

But I thought you would know it was me, too.

You know what happened next: we were ten little pins, standing in formation with our arms by our sides, chins up, eyes shut. Naked to the ball rolling end over end at us, its thumbhole spewing ash.

I was in the back row with Nickel Eye. Holding his hand.

Naitche and LP Deal were to either side of us, Back Iron and Denim Horse twinned in the second row. Behind them were Cat Stand and Courtney Peltdowne, Mary Boy between them, balancing them. Staring at the ball.

We weren't complete until you stepped into place, all alone at the front.

When you fell, I breathed in, waited for the rush of air, the crash.

First the poker game, though. Red Hat. Gooseneck calling with a sneer, Big Hair and Mary Boy looking up from the napkins they'd been keeping track on, LP Deal still writing, his pencil a nub.

'Hey,' Mary Boy said to him.

LP Deal swallowed. Put his pencil down.

Venetia smiled.

It's not like we couldn't all see their cards. Like we didn't know it had been a misdeal, a cowboy hand: that there was one black hat among all these white. One bad guy.

Gooseneck slapped his card down face-up: the seven of hearts.

He was a red Indian. He breathed out through his nose, looked to Mary Boy, a red Indian too—a king, even—and Venetia, the diamond she'd traced with her fingertips. They didn't win anything, but they didn't lose that much, either.

Naitche was at the table now, Cat Stand standing with her ball, watching him.

It was down to Big Hair and Nickel Eye and LP Deal.

Nickel Eye walked LP Deal's scratch paper over with his fingers, read aloud:

had life rotten
nod at the rifle

I saw myself in the lower panel of a comic book, leaning over, screaming, but there was no sound. It was all inside. I would have reached for him too to stop all this, but Mary Boy already was. The microphone crunched under his grip.

Denim Horse stood up out of the past, loomed over the table, the tips of his hair brushing the cards, eyes flaring. 'Who killed Coach?' he said, just like a movie Indian.

LP Deal looked up, around. 'I did,' he said finally, then to Nickel Eye: 'The fine old rat, right?'

Nickel Eye nodded, rearranging the letters on LP Deal's napkin.

He slid them over to Big Hair.

She glanced down, back up.

I was still shaking my head no.

Now Mary Boy had the napkin.

He lowered his head, pinching the bridge of his nose, his sunglasses riding up. Denim Horse ready to explode on a word, LP Deal staring up at him, waiting for it; *wanting* it.

'Shit,' Mary Boy said, though.

Gooseneck read the napkin aloud when it got to him:

end of the trail

end of the trail

It was the anagram Naitche had peeled from around his bubble gum months ago, cracked without meaning to, his arm still throbbing. One of the old anthropologist codes. What some part of LP Deal had to have known since seeing Cat Stand the first day she walked in: that Owen82 was what he was, had been doing what he had been doing. And that he had taken Owen82's place in the garden.

LP Deal reached for the card on his forehead to finish the game, but Naitche was riding his arm.

'*No*,' he was saying.

His voice was perfect.

Even the air handlers cycled down to hear it. In the new stillness a turnip vine spooled down from the rafters.

'*No*,' Naitche said again, looking hard into LP Deal's eyes, imploring, but then he was lifted away by the arm. By Cat Stand.

There was a lot of money at stake, a pile full of shells. She had a good excuse for it. And maybe his arm wouldn't even bruise this time. Not that it mattered.

LP Deal rose to her, pulling Naitche away, holding him like the child he was, and they faced off—LP Deal with the two of hearts on his forehead, Cat Stand in her wet undershirt, her breasts pressing through.

I think now she smelled like ice cream because she never stopped lactating: the sweat was her thin milk.

She looked at all of us, breathed twice through her teeth, then rolled her shirt off, threw it on the floor, her great brown breasts heaving, staring at us all.

This was the day she would bowl 300. The day Double Clutch pulled a 7/10 split in the thirteenth frame, and she held that twenty-pound ball between her full breasts, slammed it down the lane so fast the wood of his seven pin splintered, entered the grain of the ten headfirst.

LP Deal and Naitche.

Naitche was still shaking his head no, but LP Deal did it anyway, staring at Cat Stand: peeled the card off his head.

He had won the hand, guessed right: he had been the bad guy here. The white man sitting at the table with all these red Indians.

Gooseneck stood before you could react, Blue Plume. Because you weren't here for a tomato who'd been recording all of us down his sleeve, but for a thief, a truck.

Two sets of handcuffs flashed: Gooseneck's and yours.

LP Deal shrank back before Gooseneck, and then Back Iron slid gracefully down the turnip vine in full and spectacular drag: stiletto pumps, hairless legs, feather boa slung over his shoulder.

He padded to the floor in front of Gooseneck.

The only sound was Denim Horse breathing in, Gooseneck rolling his sleeves up his forearms, Back Iron smiling with his teeth together. All his old radiation had risen to the halogen whites of his eyes. He flared them, and the only thing that kept Gooseneck from doing whatever it was he could do was the boa. The white feathers. Like Smudge. Like this was all a trick, a game.

He looked to Denim Horse and then to Back Iron again, hand-cuffed Denim Horse just on principle, Back Iron singling you out, raising his wrists together, and I can tell you this now because it doesn't matter: when you pushed both of them up to the wall to see who matched the postcard, Mary Boy smiled. Because he could still redeem Owen82. He could still switch the Twin Towers out. It was the only time he ever took his sunglasses off—to squint at Back Iron and Denim Horse, give them the one who had the hair, the clothes, the look. The one you wanted.

And Eddie Dial didn't say anything, and when Denim Horse could have said no, explained it all away, he looked instead to Back

Iron, wearing a dress maybe just because his brother liked women, his brother who was perfect—had everything, didn't have to steal it—then he looked to Cat Stand *un*dressed, her breasts bare for the first time since Arizona probably, and it all felt right. Like it was his turn. He nodded with Mary Boy, that he was guilty. That he hadn't been able to run fast enough with her through the rodeo. That he had never had leukemia.

I said his name and knew you would never hold him. Not like I had, anyway.

After the line-up was over, Eddie Dial was standing there still, touching the scratches on his own face.

It sucks being Indian sometimes, okay, but sometimes, too

I couldn't finish it, didn't have enough words.

Instead I just wrote *I'm losing myse*

LP Deal didn't collect the money, drag it with him to the bathroom. But they hadn't forgotten about him, just didn't know how to get him out.

And the whole time, Cat Stand kept bowling.

We were all watching, frame by frame.

This is where I brush up against you in line. It's when you've got Denim Horse cuffed in front of you. Because he wanted a drink. Because this wasn't America—he had rights. You had caught your man, done in twenty minutes what I hadn't in twenty days. And Courtney Peltdowne was right behind you, and I grabbed your arm and you looked at my blonde hair and my red eyes and didn't know me, shrugged me away, and she laughed too long, and you turned to her, smiling yourself.

And I'm glad for you and her. Really (lie). Have a bunch of kids. Name them after me: Tie Rod, Drive Shaft, Rear End; Spindle Boy, Spindle Girl.

A third set of cuffs caught the light, then: mine.

You must have known me then, when I joined you and her at the wrist, Denim Horse smiling, the wind catching his hair, like he was already running.

But it doesn't matter.

I didn't look back.

Gooseneck knew I was undercover now, let me walk into the bathroom first. Because it was the women's. Because I knew him, LP Deal.

I think I was supposed to give him a way out, too. Let him run, feel it, then shoot him right then. It was going to be mercy.

But I knew him.

Or thought I did.

I just wanted to rearrange the pins, I think, put all the sound back in them, stand them up very still and walk away. But this was Fool's Hip. The walls of the bathroom were crumbling, Cat Stand and Double Clutch hammering the AllSkin tournament into history.

In the middle of it all were LP Deal and Naitche.

In the toilets and smoking in the trashcan were all of LP Deal's notebooks. To keep them from the anthropologists. The only one I'd be able to salvage would be his unfinished manifesto, the terms he was dictating to America—transcriptions of clippings from newspapers and history books, done up in alphabetical order, like entries in a dictionary. It was written on the back of an aborted series of profiles he'd written on Mary Boy and Back Iron and Denim Horse and Cat Stand and Nickel Eye and Owen82 and himself. Written back when they were all suspects. And he was first, had been the one standing over the body with the gun.

The wall behind them was open, too.

The lockers.

Back Iron's contraband.

LP Deal reached around it for the AllSkin robe and wrapped Naitche in it, holding it together at the throat for him, showing him *how*, then placed Nickel Eye's golden helmet on his head, ran facefirst into the wall again and again, until he was bleeding from the eyes, until the chink in the cinderblock opened enough to allow a small body.

Naitche.

LP Deal pulled him close. Behind them something else clattered down in stages: a pipe bundle. The Freak Pipe. I stepped in with them, held it on my forearm like you're supposed to, handed it to Naitche. He took it like he knew what it was, what it held. And maybe he did.

He blinked his eyes in goodbye and I blinked back, and then LP Deal pushed him through and collapsed, the better part of him stumbling into the light, and I had to see, *see* it better, so I pushed out the door, past Gooseneck, and found the stairs to the roof by instinct, spiraled up them four at a time, burst out into the open.

Enil Anderson was there.

My pistol flashed down my arm, to my hand, between me and him, and the world rotated around us for a few breaths.

He was smiling, his skin drawn and leathery, and crowding all around us were the other thirty-nine, and I couldn't spin fast enough. And the smell.

I don't know the name of the one I finally shot, but she didn't care: they were dead. Mounted on crossed poles, their eyes sewn open.

American scarecrows.

The one I shot was still spinning, smiling.

My pistol clattered to the roof.

This was a holy place.

I took off my shoes and walked through them, pushing off from body to body, and they were whispering about *Naitche, Naitche, Naitche*, and the Special Agent who had been Chassis Jones breathed in and leaned over the edge of Fool's Hip for a last first glimpse of him, weaving himself into the yellow grass. He was growing smaller and smaller, and in the shimmering instant he became for her a buffalo calf she breathed in and became part of it, like Back Iron, like Nickel Eye, like Bacteen, and the tipi rings stories below her rose into hoops of ash, so she could walk through them, the first one taking her wig, the second her sunglasses, the third her name, and the fourth issuing her a pair of dingy canvas shoes, and then she was looking up, past Naitche and the man waiting for him on the horse, into the sky, and it was empty, like a bowl spilled then righted again, waiting to be filled.

Behind her the katsina in the olive green jacket leaned down to his tied hand, for a cigarette; smiled. This is the way it is: after the massacres and after the cigar stores, we gathered around the fire, told stories and watched each other's faces for signs of ourselves.

It was a third world country, but we called it the first.

It was a good day to die, but nobody did.

is this how it begins?

yes.

abergeny— *adj., arch., colloq.* INDIAN.

Bacteen (bak´ tēn)— **1.** the mendicant barber –*n*. **2.** holdover from the pre-CONSERVATION days, when INDIANS still cut their hair –*n*.

Barefoot No Guns— famous INDIAN martial artist.

big chief— **1.** methylenedioxymethamphetamine –*n., Pharm.* **2.** a big, red tablet –*n., colloq.*

Blackhawk's Revenge— **1.** anorexia nervosa –*n., euph.* **2.** what some Americans claim to have 'caught' from looking at photographs of INDIANS of the Reservation Era –*n*.

BLM— *n., Organis.* Bureau of Land Management.

border— **1.** no man's land between America and the INDIAN TERRITO-RIES –*n., Geog.* **2.** where you exile TOMATOES –*n*. **Syn. 1.** redline, fringe, strip, brink, track, supercollider, new medicine line, hardline, end of the end of the trail. **2.** RMZ. **3.** the looking glass.

Brasscalves— **1.** IHS-sponsored fitness club and resale shop *–n., Estab.* **2.** the first of the INDIAN businesses to barter for dues *–n.*

Bright Eyes— my old name.

BTLS— **1.** Born Too Late Syndrome *–n., Psychol.* **2.** a psychosomatic condition *–n., Pathol.*

Bush Whacker— sullen trickster of *SUSANNAH OF THE MOUNTIES*, played of course by Long Lance.

cat stand— *n., arch.* nineteenth-century slang for roadside bordello.

Charity Stripers— *n., pl.* pep-squad for the WARRIORS, the premiere INDIAN basketball team of the TERRITORIES.

chassis jones— *n., Psychol.* the distinct and undeniable need for a frame. [back-formation from 'basketball jones,' 'cigarette jones,' etc.]

Code— **1.** the pamphlet distributed to all INDIANS at the BORDER, as condition of entry *–n.* **2.** a cultural primer or guidebook on INDIAN etiquette *–n., Socio.*

Columbus Day— *n., Hist.* 21 May.

Conservation Act— *n., Hist.* the accidental solution to the 'Indian Problem' (under pressure from Keep America Beautiful, the American Congress signed into law an aggressive bill requiring 'the restoration of all indigenous flora and fauna to the Great Plains.' As wildlife biologists soon pointed out, though, for a disturbance-dependent landscape to regain anything approaching self-sufficiency—to say nothing of momentum—the reintroduced grass (*buchloë dactyloides*) needed buffalo (*bison bison*) to 'disturb' it, and, just as the prairie dog (*cynomys ludovicianus*) needed the disturbance of the blackfooted ferrett (*mustela nigripes*), so did the burgeoning herds of reintroduced buffalo need the INDIAN (*canis latrans*)).

cowdrops— *n., pl., Pharm.* mild livestock tranquilizers popular before IHS reformed.

Daily Bison— *n., Perio.* irregular, independent newspaper popular in the TERRITORIES.

'dance'— what Clark said to his black 'manservant' York, in spite of his frostbitten penis.

Day of the Dead— *n., Hist.* ten months after the CONSERVATION ACT and the resulting SKIN PARADE (i.e., the winter after the GREAT PLAINS FIRE), the North American INDIAN population doubled and then halved just as fast, the outskirts of town silent as the women walked out into the grass with decorated shoeboxes, their stillborn children who, according to news accounts, rose up from their cradleboard caskets the following spring as buffalo.

diabetes— *n., Pathol.* as Eddie Dial says: 'when I can smell the sugar in my urine, I know then that I'm my father's son, that I'm INDIAN.'

dogs of war— *n., Socio.* rising from the stew.

Double Dog— *n.* famous INDIAN daredevil.

Downward Facing Dog— 1. famous Coeur d'Alene yogi (not to be confused with Side Crow).

factory defects— *n., pl.* what each package of OCCAM'S RAZORS came with: depressions on each side, for thumb and forefinger, and an instruction booklet detailing the dangers of cutting longwise up the arterial vein in your wrist, chewing aspirin, and soaking in warm water well out of reach of the telephone, the neighbors, IHS. Diagrams were included. They were in color (red).

Fat Deer Hilton— 1. American hunting resort located in the TERRITORIES —*n., Estab.* 2. another 'end of the trail' anagram –*n.*

firing line— *n., Myth.* what NATTY COOPER is supposed to have laughed at when there was nobody there to even hear.

Fool's Hip— *n., Estab.* minor bowling alley in Former South Dakota (was *Ship of Fools* until Mary Boy sold the name but didn't invest the money in a new sign, just told his itinerant, iliterate maintenance man to rearrange the letters into *Fools' Ship*, which is roughly when he added all the superfluous spelling and essay questions to the backside of his application for employment, questions for which LP DEAL was absolutely made).

Freak Pipe— *n.* the Holy Grail.

full-blood— *n., Pathol.* approximately eight pints.

gauche (gōsh)— *adj. Fr.* for 'left,' as in 'gone.'

Geronimo— *interj.* what Crazy Horse didn't say.

Ghost Dance— *n., Hist.* late nineteenth-century effort to 'restore all indigenous flora and fauna to the Great Plains.'

Gulag (gōō´ läg)— *n., euph.* what the dishwashers call the sprawling, stainless steel kitchen of the MAYFLOWER.

Guneaters Anonymous— *n., Organis.* a euphemism.

Happy Hour— *n., Hist.* unofficial name of the big drunk that started with the RED ALERT and ended on the first DAY OF THE DEAD. The eighth of the population that didn't die of alcohol poisoning died driving home from the bar.

happy hunting grounds— *n., Geog., Psychol.* the fifteenth century.

Hemogoblin (hē´ mə gob´ lin)— **1.** recklessly edited junior-high life-science film in which the militaristic white blood cells fall victim to an animated retrovirus, leaving the red blood cells alone in the bloodstream at long last *–n., Biochem.* **2.** an underground classic *–n., Socio.*

homesteaders— *n.* those Americans who moved onto the reservations after the PENNIES DOWN frenzy.

Hudson's— *n., Estab.* 'the indigenous grocery store.'

Huna Deal— *n., Hist.* the controversial land exchanges immediately following the CONSERVATION ACT where the total acreage of the temporarily 'abandoned' reservations was traded for BLM land immediately surrounding the TERRITORIES, sometimes at the request of the tribe or nation, but, in the case of some of the tribes or nations holding land bordering national parks, without consent, too. *see also:* PENNIES DOWN SYNDROME

IHS— *n., Estab.* Indian Health Services.

Indiamen— **1.** fleet of unlicensed truck drivers who make daily supply runs between the INDIAN TERRITORIES and the SATELLITE RESERVATIONS *–n., Occup., pl.* **2.** any truck driven, pushed or pulled by INDIAMEN *–n., colloq.*

Indian (in´ dē ən)— *adj.* a mode of dress which peaked when eleven-year-old Norseman Leif Garrett walked onto the production stage of *The Dating Game* wearing beads and buckskin. The girls in the front row screamed and plain fainted. They were all INDIAN.

Indian Burn— **1.** the Great Plains Fire, claimed to be the 'only first [sic] INDIAN act visible from space *–n.* **2.** often cited as one of the early instances of Reverse Blanket Warfare *–n., colloq. see also:* TWO BURN FLAT

Indian Head Penny— *n., Psychol.* the Oneida woman who went through eight marathon cosmetic surgeries to fit the classic one-cent profile.

Indian Territories— **1.** no longer just Oklahoma *–n., Geog.* **2.** not made of milk and honey *–n.* **Syn. 1.** INDIANation, Brave Red World, New New World, 'Home on the Range,' Red Earth, Red Spot, Red Sea, Rouge City, SAVAGE Kingdom, INDIAN Ocean, 'Cities of the Plain,' 'INDIAN America.' **2.** in the words of the defunct *Dakota*

Star, 'one big, honking red light district.' **Usage:** often shortened to 'TERRITORIES' in MISCHIF.

ivory trade— *n., Hist.* ushered in the CONSERVATION Era.

Judas stock— *n., Socio.* the individual horse, cow, buffalo, sheep or pig trained to lead the rest of the herd (flock, etc.) to slaughter, usually distinguished either by copper bells or special favor and referred to as 'Judas horse, Judas cow,' etc. *see also: LP DEAL*

Karma (kär´mə)— *n., Relig.* why on the morning the CONSERVATION ACT was voted into law, the majority of the dissenting Congressmen's alarm clocks failed to ring, due to power failures. The rest were tied to their beds with their own sheets. One had inhaled a whiffle ball. The SKIN PARADE had already started by the time he coughed it up.

'keep off the grass'— **1.** what Enil Anderson painted on signs every workday for six years *–phras.* **2.** what America says to INDIANS – *imper.*

KLIM (klim)— **1.** 'the extremist band' *–n., colloq.* **2.** 'the last hostile station on the FM' *–n., colloq.* **3.** 'milk,' backwards, on purpose.

late movie— *n. The Scraeling.*

Lily Deer— *n.* the 'Native advice columnist.'

Little America— **1.** the vast, fast-food district of New Bismarck *–n., Geog.* **1.** the fast-food section of any town, or food court of any mall *–n., colloq.*

Lovelocks'— **1.** a chain of INDIAN hair salons / embassies in America *–n., Estab.* **2.** supposed to be BACTEEN's former place of employment *–n., Myth.*

LP Deal— **1.** 'long-play deal' *–n.* **2.** six letters still visible on an abandoned record store window on the abergeny side of the BORDER *–n., Hist.*

Lunar Boy Hoax— *n., Hist.* the valiant, pre-CONSERVATION effort by NATTY COOPER to 'restore all indigenous flora and fauna to the Great Plains' by intimating over a live SATELLITE feed that there was gold on the moon, prompting a nightly series of 'Yellowside Reports' which culminated in a brief resurgence of interest in the space program (see: funding); though only five Americans (one shuttle crew) left before the rush was over, many credit NATTY COOPER with setting the stage for CONSERVATION.

Magpie & Muskrat— *n., Entert.* pair of combative, resilient cartoon characters.

Manifest Destiny— *n.* star of *SUSANNAH OF THE MOUNTIES*, known both for her willingness and her vocal range. *see also: VIRGINIA DARE*

Maryland— *n., Estab.* Catholic amusement park.

Mary Rowlandson— *n.* still tied up, and liking it.

Mayflower— casino-resort just inside the TERRITORIES –*n., Estab.* **2.** major American getaway –*n., Touris.*

Mischif— *n., Ling.* (re)combination of all the major language groups into a constantly-shifting, perpetually evasive pan-INDIAN vernacular.

Miss Dick—**1.** *n., Entert.* a professional nomad (amateur fugitive). **2.** *n., Entert.* stage name for the popular new sleuth in the traveling *SUSANNAH OF THE MOUNTIES* production, often billed as 'Miss America's new roommate.'

morion (môr´ē on´)— *n., Hist.* helmet fashionable among 17th century conquistadors.

Narcisco Borjoques— *n., Hist.* California bandit of the 1860s who shot each of his victims once, through the head (not to be confused with Joaquin Murieta).

Natty Cooper— **1.** a martyr –*n.* **2.** the first INDIAN on the moon / original LUNAR BOY –*n., Bio.* **3.** was made a posthumous holy clown for whispering 'gold' into his headset to the American audience, then hopping away forty feet at a time, hiding for three oxygen-rich (lunar) days in which he's supposed to have consorted and cavorted with imperialist Martians, trading military secrets and traditional recipes –*n., Entert.* **3.** was ultimately fined 28.2 *billion* dollars by a temporary consortium of television networks and federal space programs, which he tried to pay in wildly irregular installments of rancid beef, glass beads, and IOU notes –*n., Legis.* **4.** assassinated en route to the TERRITORIES by American PATRIOTS dressed up as redcoats –*n., Hist.* **Syn. 1.** 'Gnat Man' **2.** 'Coop.'

New World Times— *n., Perio.* 'the indigenous newspaper.'

Nickel Eye, or, **Nikolai** (nik´ə lī)— **1.** claims his father was so INDIAN he would hunt deer with tennis balls, just to make it even – *n.* **2.** likely from one of the SATELLITE RESERVATIONS –*n.*

No More Promises, No More Lies— *n., Entert.* popular soap opera (not to be confused with *Young Pagans in Love* or *The Grass Still Grows* or *All My Relations* or *And the River Flowed*).

non-dairy creamer— *n., colloq.* MANIFEST DESTINY.

Norman's Invasion— *n., Hist.* the border scuffle brought on by Norman Pease and his white eyes when they tried to immigrate to the TERRITORIES at YAQUI BUOY.

Occam's Razor— **1.** 'for the INDIAN in you' –*n., Socio.* **2.** an import –*n.*

one and five-sixteenths— *phras.* how INDIAN NICKEL EYE says he is.

'Oral History of Buffaloes'— *n., Liter.* the shortest of LP DEAL's *esc(r)apegoat* notebooks (full text: *it was nice, and then They came*).

parfleche (pär ˊ flĕsh ˊ)—**1.** a bag made from rough hide that's had the hair removed, more or less –*n.* **2.** a woman's least favorite purse –*n., Fashio.*

passenger pigeon— **1.** a large bird with red eyes, of the family Columbidae (*ectopistes migratorius*), which once 'roamed the virgin forests of North America in unbelievable numbers' –*n., Cryptozoo., Hist.* **2.** according to Audubon, a bird 'steered by a long well-plumed tail, and propelled by well-set wings, the muscles of which are very large and powerful for the size of the bird. When an individual is seen gliding through the woods and close to the observer, it passes like a thought, and on trying to see it again, the eye searches in vain. The bird is gone.' –*n., Lit. see also:* VANISHING INDIANS

Patriots— *n., org.* short-lived ragtag band of hardline conservative Americans who routinely dressed up in various period costumes and snuck across the BORDER to take political prisoners, each of whom was summarily found guilty and executed in whatever manner went with the costumes; 'short-lived' because when they dressed up like INDIANS once, their sister-organization in the TERRITORIES happened to be dressed up like cowboys, specifically, a posse of John Wayne's many characters. The Duke smiled, crossed his arms over the saddle horn, and pushed his hat up with the barrel of his pistol, all this long black hair spilling out.

pemmican (pĕm ˊ ĭ kən)— **1.** dried meat pounded into a paste with whatever's left over in the bottom drawer of the refrigerator –*n.* **2.** has a shelf life of five years –*n., Myth.* **3.** potted meat, without the pot –*n., colloq.*

Pennies Down Syndrome— *n., Pathol.* vacant stare associated with those INDIANS who returned home after HAPPY HOUR to find Americans living in their homes, courtesy of the HUNA DEAL, which auctioned their 'abandoned' land for 'pennies on the dollar.'

pet coyote— *n.,* MISCHIF for recreational peyote [*pet* + *coyote*].

pink eye— *n.*, *Pharm.*, *Pathol.*, *Socio.* all the rage.

piskun— *n.*, *arch.*, when buffalo act like lemmings (not to be confused with COWDROPS).

Red Alert— *n.*, *Hist.*, *phras.* the now-historic initial radio report that the CONSERVATION ACT had passed, that 'the Dakotas were INDIAN again.'

Red Dawn— **1.** video reenactment of the SKIN PARADE –*n.*, *colloq.*, **2.** delayed visual for the GHOST DANCE –*n.*, *Hist.* **3.** what LUNAR BOY had to be seeing when he looked down at the earth and whispered 'gold' –*n.*, *Myth.*

Red Hat— *n.* variation of Indian Poker; a game of logic with four or more people and a deck of cards, the object being to deduce if you have the 'red' card stuck to your forehead or not (in misdealt all 'red' hands, it's played as if it's 'Black Hat'—i.e., the goal is to deduce if you're wearing the 'black hat' at the table with all these 'red' INDIANS, i.e., if you have the lowbelly card, if you're 'white').

Red Hat Trick— *n.* to see what you can't see. **Syn. 1.** medicine hat.

Red Matters— *n.* the only political talk show to use a gong.

RMZ— *n.*, *Geog.* re-militarized zone.

Rubber Glove of God— *n.*, *Entert.* the traveling SUSANNAH OF THE MOUNTIE's variation of a minor BACTEEN riff (not to be confused with '*Make Him Dance*' or '*The Latterday Coup Machine*' or '*Pale Young Four Toes*' or '*The Unphallic Tale of the Woodpecker*' or '*Tongues of Dung*' or '*No More Beads*' or '*The Best of All Possible Worlds*' or '*The Only Good INDIANS*' or '*Subterranean Iron Horse Blues*' or '*A Particularly Articulate War Cry*').

satellite reservations— *n.*, *pl.* used for farming elk, sage, tobacco, etc.

Savage (sav´ ij)— *n.*, *Liter.* opera about a Yamana-man traded as an infant for a shiny button. He grows up to kill eight Europeans on a missionary boat.

security gourds— *n.*, *pl.* 'emit a shrill whistle when anyone approaches.'

Seventh Cavalry— **1.** the WASHINGTON GENERALS of the clan league –*n.*, *Sport.* **2.** composed mostly of ex-rodeo clowns and professional eaters *n.*, *Socio.*

Shanghai Lil— **1.** never used the pill –*n.* **2.** named for her epicanthic folds –*n.* **3.** Navajo-Havasupai-(Mennonite-) German performance artist whose career spanned from the Brief Indian Awakening (*The*

Scraeling) to Conservation (*SUSANNAH OF THE MOUNTIES*) –*n.* **4.** indomitable –*n.*

Sheep Belly— **1.** an INDIAN Nobody –*n.* **2.** a minor trickster –*n.*, *Socio.*

shy boy— *n.* LP DEAL.

Sitting Duck— *n.*, *Entert.* the INDIAN Lenny Bruce.

Skin & Bones— *n.* a children's game where they lower their heads and hump their backs up like buffalo, then wait for whoever's 'it' to shoot them, skin them, and leave their bones. But then they rise up singing, are all 'it' now, give chase to the hunter. *see also: DAY OF THE DEAD*

Skin Pageant— *n.*, *Socio.* where you figure out who Miss America isn't.

Skin Parade— **1.** the mass exodus following the RED ALERT –*n. Hist.* **2.** a chain of topless bars in Florida, America –*n.* **Syn. 1.** Red Tide, RED DAWN, Red Shift; Red Cloud, Red Wind, Red Scare, Relocation.

Slugpusher— **1.** the bartender in a gin joint –*n.* **2.** a gunslinger –*n.* **3.** BACTEEN's side-armed, side-whiskered all-American sidekick. –*n.*, *Myth.*

Split Feather— **1.** adopted name of ex-Olympic Menominee gymnast who led the first piskun of Indian Days –*n.*, *Hist.* **2.** typically depicted leaning forward, out of the frame, running ahead of uncounted tons of salvation. –*n.*, *Art.*

Springheel Jack— *n.*, *Sport.* a WAR GOD.

Sun Dogs— *n.*, *Sport.* dominant bowlers of the clan league.

Susannah of the Mounties— **1.** *n.*, *Entert.* underground stag movie popular in the TERRITORIES, based on the 1939 National Telefilm Association movie starring Shirley Temple and Randolph Scott, where 'Shirley ('Susannah Seldon') is the orphaned survivor of an INDIAN attack in the Canadian West. A Mountie named 'Monty' (Scott) and his girlfriend take her in. Everybody suffers further INDIAN attacks and the Mountie is saved from the stake only by Shirley's 'intervention' with the INDIAN chief (John Big Tree).'

Sweeney Todd— **1.** serial-killing barber –*n.*, *Liter.* **2.** BACTEEN's nom de plume when visiting America –*n.*, *Myth.*

tabula rosa (tab´ yə lə rōsə)— **1.** 'red slate' –*nomin.*, *colloq.* **2.** anthropological term for one who's sufficiently brainwashed to be a TOMATO –*n.* **Syn. 1.** indios blanco (not to be confused with apples).

tan lines— *n.* what the Lone Ranger had to have.

telepawn— **1.** to call the Aborigine Hotline –*v.* **2.** to sell your soul to the devil –*v., colloq.*

Thorpes (thôrp)— **1.** track and field athletes –*n., pl.* **2.** hard to catch –*n., pl.*

tiospaye (tē´ ō shpā)— **1.** who you run with –*n., colloq.* **2.** your extended family –*n.*

tomato— *n.* red on the outside *and* the in-, yet white just the same.

Tom Starr— *n., Hist.* tall tall Cherokee man b. 1813, purported to have killed more than one hundred people.

toughest chickens—*phras.* never had their internal chickens plucked.

travois (trə´ voi)— **1.** a wheel-less cart you tie behind your horse, dog, whatever –*n., colloq.* **2.** anything you tie behind your horse, dog, car, etc., with the intention of transporting something in or upon it –*n., colloq.*

trick— *n., colloq.* what the older generation told us the SKIN PARADE was: a TRICK to get all the INDIANS in one place. The Gatling gun they imagined was huge, locked in a geostationary orbit somewhere over the Great Plains.

Two Burn Flat— *n., Geog.* the barren, ashen region surrounding FOOL'S HIP.

Two Guns White Calf— *n.* the original copper INDIAN, used now to market PuriTan sunbathing products.

Two Little Indians— *n., Entert.* the MAGPIE & MUSKRAT show.

Urban Elk— *n., Sport.* the SUN DOGS' traditional opposition.

Vanishing Indians— **1.** masters of camouflage –*n.* **2.** a troupe of nomadic heyokas best known for fortifying YAQUI BUOY against NORMAN'S INVASION by constructing a leering papier-mâché coyote large enough to straddle the road –*n., Hist.*

Virginia Dare— *n., Hist.* led the SKIN PARADE.

War Gods— *n., Sport.* those WARRIORS who have had their jerseys retired and bundled.

Warriors— *n., Sport.,* what Denim Horse and Back Iron should have been. **Syn. 1.** Red Giants.

Wasee Maza— *Hist.* said of Wounded Knee: 'when I saw all those little infants lying there dead in their blood, my feeling was that even if I *ate* one of the soldiers, it would not appease my anger.'

Wash Board— *n., Sport.* hereditary name of a line of Inuit bodybuilders.

Washington Generals— *n.* Sherman, Sheridan, Cooke, etc.

Waymon Tise— *n.* categorically denies his role in the SKIN PARADE (of discovering the loophole in the CONSERVATION ACT which simply specified 'fauna,' which, as he noted in a public radio interview, *could* legally entail INDIANS, as we were still on the books with mountain lions and coyotes as 'varmints,' *bounty*).

X-Rays— *n., pl.* the only way to look at some of the old bundles.

Yaqui Buoy (yä´ kē boi)— *n.* the first tollbooth to achieve mythological status.

Year of the Cat— *n., Hist.* this one.

ARTEFACTS

ITEM 1: FBI MEMO 32.B-197 M ('THE HARRIS DETAIL.'), BADLY MIS-DATED (DUE TO POOR REPRODUCTION)

Though none of Mary Boy's peyote-dispensing federal agents seemed to have distinguished themselves by their height (p.21; cf. pp. 61, 90 and 105-6), nevertheless, versions of this recently-released document still surface on a regular basis to support his claim.

The handwritten portion '4' reads:

We have / ████ photos / of ████ in the Canadienne / league, trying to revive his / basketball career, if you need them. Please note (Harris) that these photos / are NOT *████ ████ from his hi- / school yrbook. Look at the* DATES *, / gentlemen, not the lapels. And any / correspondence to Agent ████ , / just address it to me. I'll see / that he gets it.*

The handwritten portion '5' reads:

And yes, the / ████████ / has been corrected. / As you have now / been.

Perhaps part of the appeal of this memo is that, according to the Mayan calendar(s), 'December 23rd, 2012' (presumably a decayed '12/23/72') is supposedly the end of this world, the beginning of the next.

Rapid City
████████████████
SD 192-329
‾‾‾‾‾‾‾‾‾‾‾‾‾‾‾‾‾‾‾‾‾‾‾‾‾‾‾‾‾‾‾‾
MARCUS TRELAWNEY ████ █
DP
SD 1400
‾‾‾‾‾‾‾‾‾‾‾‾‾‾‾‾‾‾‾‾‾‾‾‾‾‾‾‾‾‾‾‾
DP
‾‾‾‾‾‾‾‾‾‾‾‾‾‾‾‾‾‾‾‾‾‾‾‾‾‾‾‾‾‾‾‾

re: ████████████ & c.n. ██████████

Three things, guys:

1) Agent █████████████ ('Stork') did NOT just 'step into the
ether of Pine Ridge SD', as the ████████████ has been reporting.
I'm talking to you here, Harris.

2) We were there. What HAPPENED was the ████████████ buttons were
sweating in the heat, and Stork neglected to wear his latex.
Meaning the psycho████████ agent ████████ ████ 3-████penetrated
the skin of his palm. And we all know what happens then.

3) What DID happen to Stork, what DOES explain his current
absence, is simple: he went AWOL. (not 'Native,' Harris, AWOL)
The ████████ ████████ 3-███ went to his head as it's designed to,
and, as that type trip ('religious experience') has yet to be
cleared for Caucasians, he had an adverse psychotic reaction.
What you saw wasn't a skinny-███ man in a 52XL suit walking
behind a tree and never emerging, but a particularly lean field
agent rigorously trained in ████████ and ████████ ████████
████████ ████████ sloping off behind a tree, then making a
ninety-degree turn, keeping that tree between you and him until
he made it to Canada.

ITEM 2: FIRST GENERATION TRANSCRIPTION OF DIGITALLY -RECOV -
ERED PORTION OF SIDE B, AUDIO CASSETTE 56.T-182 I.B ('T HIRD PRIZE')

As the last 'definition' for 'Border' (the fifth entry in the 'Terms')
suggests, 'tomatoes' are to be deposited at the border between the
Indian Territories and America-proper, which is of course strictly in
keeping with traditional patterns of Native American justice, which,
in the absence of any form of capital punishment, insist instead upon
banishment, or exile, to the point that this forced absence of community or any social and/or familial bonds is actually perceived to be
worse than death itself.

The complication, of course, isn't on the part of the exiled—in this
case, LP Deal (RM-5454-21), evidently still talking into his wrist-mi-
crophone (in the women's restroom of p.155)—but on the guards
themselves, who are put in the position the 'tomatoes' have been in
all along: they've been assigned to deliver (one of) their people to the
anthropologists. But they've been culturally conditioned away from
just such an act. At this point they would seem to have only two
options: enforce the banishment by delivering the 'tomato,' thus betraying their culture (as anthropologists are, to them, the distillation
of all that America is or has been), or *not* deliver the 'produce,' thus
risking both their own employment *and* the guaranteed further be-
trayals the 'tomato' will commit if allowed to remain inside the Indian Territories. However, over the years a third option has presented
itself: carelessness; ineptitude. The guards drive for the border as
they've been directed, only; first, forgetting the most direct route—
'taking the long way there'—and, second, 'accidentally' leaving a host
of donated goods in the back of the windowless van for their traitor:
ropes, pills, belts, shoestrings. Sometimes just a door that unlocks at
seventy miles per hour. Because they're wearing handcuffs, the 'tomatoes' have to turn around to open the door, nod thanks to the
guards, their hair whipping in their eyes.

Of the two former guards interviewed about this so far (AH-9199
and ▮▮▮▮▮), neither have any comments on these small acts of
'mercy' (their word), but choose instead to stare out the window of
their respective cells, a song rising in their throats for the morning.

3:10r [SOMETHING ABOUT HORSES?] ... BUT HER I CAN ASK FOR
IT TO BE HER IN THE VAN AND ~~MAYBE~~ MAYBE
EVEN HIM THOUGH I DON'T KNOW BUT AT ~~THE~~

3:13r LEAST HER BECAUSE SHE'S INDIAN SHE'LL
LEAVE ~~THAT~~ THE DOOR UNLOCKED FOR ME
AND NOT WATCH IN THE REARVIEW MIRROR
JUST KEEP HER HANDS ON THE WHEEL AND
BECAUSE SHE'S INDIAN SHE'LL ~~PROBABLY~~ GO FASTER

3:17r TO MAKE IT EASY TO MAKE IT QUICK BECAUSE SHE'S
INDIAN SHE'LL LET ME [unclear; 3sec] AND MAYBE
SHE WILL LOOK BACK OR I'LL LEAN UP AND LACE MY
FINGERS INTO THE STEEL [sic] WIRE BETWEEN THE
DRIVER'S SEAT AND THE PASSENGER'S AND MAKE HER

3:20r LOOK BACK ASK HER WITHOUT HAVING TO REALLY
SAY IT [?] TOUCH THE BACK OF MY FINGERS WITH
THE BACK OF HERS BUT SHE HAS TO KEEP HER
HANDS ON THE WHEEL TOO BECAUSE WHEN I
SLIDE THE DOOR BACK THE VAN WILL TRY TO

3:21r PULL THAT WAY INTO THE GRASSLANDS TOO
[B/C IT'S "INDIAN" TOO?] BUT IT'S NOT HER THAT
HAS TO STEP OUT IT'S ME IT'S ME IT'S
ME I JUST WANT TO FEEL THE HEADS

3:24r OF THE GRASS BRUSHING UNDER THE
THIN SOLES OF MY SHOES FOR A FEW
MOMENTS IF I CAN. BECAUSE MAYBE I
CAN WALK ON THEM. MAYBE WE ALL
CAN

Printed in the United States
96397LV00002B/193-291/A